Voices from the Susquehanna: Harford County's Newest Writers

A Collection of Diverse Fiction and Non-Fiction by New Maryland Writers

Edited by Ted M. Zurinsky
Illustrated by Robin Wintz

Published by Rocky Waters Publishing Group

Copyright 2005

TABLE OF CONTENTS

THE HOMESTEADERS, Karin Harrison....................5

IT'S A GREAT DAY FOR FLYING, K. Kellogg Smith..........16

GROWING UP COLD…, Lu Maistros.................20

SEARCHERS IN THE MIST, Charlotte R. Wrublewski..........28

ORANGE CRUSH, Lois Gilbert.......................36

BALANCE, Ted M. Zurinsky.........................40

HOPE IN THE ATTIC, Mary Beth Creighton.............47

HEARING…LOST AND FOUND, Lois Gilbert..................52

TERROR IN THE BARN, Ann M. Cook..........................58

RAIN, Danny L. Imwold...............................64

REBER'S POND, Ann M. Cook...............................72

DANCING WITH SARA, Lois Gilbert...........................82

ARCANUM, James A. Vella.............................85

A GIFT FOR BENJAMIN, Ann M. Cook........................95

A LITTLE CHILD…, JoAnn M. Macdonald.....................110

GENTLEMEN: START YOUR ENGINES, Lu Maistros……..118

THE SORREL MULES, Ann M. Cook..........................124

HUNTER, Danny L. Imwold..........................140

THE DEEP CREEK ROD AND GUN CLUB..., Frank Soul...149

A LIGHT DUSTING OF SNOW, Mary Beth Creighton……...155

HARRY AND GOLDIE, Lu Maistros...............................182

Authors: Biographies and Writing Backgrounds..................192

THE HOMESTEADERS

by

Karin Harrison

The dry desert wind jostles the tumbleweed, whistling through its tightly woven mesh. The sympathetic wind seems to moan and sweeps over the three children huddled together, staring silently at the heap of red clay covered with broken rocks. A small cross fashioned by little hands and pirated from the broken spokes of a wagon wheel and clumsily tied together with heavy rope proclaims this as hallowed ground. Tattered remnants of brightly colored hair ribbons tied around the lone marker tremble in the breeze.

Maggie is reading the twenty-third psalm from a frayed bible while keeping a firm grip on Rosebud's apron. Jenny rests her head on Maggie's shoulder and stares vacantly. The screeching sound of a vulture hopping expectantly nearby prompts Jenny to turn, give chase, and scream at the uninvited guest. The large bird, awkward and clumsy on the ground, takes flight, his huge wings swishing through the late afternoon sky. Jenny comes to an abrupt stop. The broken-down wagon is resting on its side; their belongings are scattered as if discarded by some frantic and frustrated thief. She stares at the bloody trail leading from the wagon to the graveside.

"Jen, we are not finished here."

Maggie gestures for Jenny to come back to join them.

"I'm hungry." Rosebud buries her face in her sister's dust-covered flannel skirt, muffling her whimpers.

Maggie closes the bible and takes a deep breath. They are alone now. What will become of them? Why did God take Papa and Mamma? Without Papa's guidance they will surely perish. She puts her arms tightly around her sisters who are weeping in near silence. They are depending on her now. Somehow she must find a way to keep them safe. She recalls her father's deep voice and somehow he is talking to her now, "Maggie, you must move on. You can do it. You are strong. Save yourselves."

She raises her head defiantly, green eyes blazing, her square jaw firmly set. She silently vows to survive and reach the lush lands of Oregon to realize Papa's dream. Whatever it takes, they will get there. She wipes her eyes and her dirty hands paint muddy trails on her cheeks. Only four months ago they left their home in Missouri. Despite his wife's frailty, Jeremiah Perrin made plans to move his family to Oregon. His family was growing and their farmland was meager and crops poor. His brother, Joseph, told in enthusiastic letters of the verdant virgin farmlands in the west. His three daughters Maggie, fourteen; Jenny, twelve; and Rosebud, just turned seven, were excited and looked forward to this adventure. He sold his property and the family embarked on the long journey in the spring of 1844.

Maggie recalls the bright sunny day when the wagon train crossed the Missouri River. It took several days for all the wagons to be ferried across. The dusty, rutted trail rocked the pioneers and the motion of the wagon made everyone sick. Sylvia, her mother who was four months pregnant, suffered the most and tried to endure the hard travel by lying on bags and blankets in the wagon. Eventually they overcame the seasick motion. The train made steady headway except for one occasion when they were surprised by an Indian raid. Fortunately, the attackers were only after food. They drove off several head of cattle and never returned.

Crossing the Platte River, the oxen lost their footing across a bank and the wagon turned over. Her mother was critically injured. She suffered a miscarriage and died that evening. They buried her near the riverbank. The girls picked wildflowers and placed them on her grave.

Steady rain pounded the wagons for days. The dampness invaded everything. Nevertheless, the wagons moved forward. Cholera became a silent assassin and the bodies of its victims were often hastily and shallowly buried on the side of the trail. At first, Jeremiah tried to shield the girls from the gruesome sight of graves dug up by animals with the scattered human bones and body parts. Eventually, these sightings proved too numerous to fret over the effects on the girls. Death became familiar.

The people on the wagon train, too, became familiar and the children made friends and reveled in the brief play period allowed after supper as they gathered around the fire. The friendships were often brief as many children died from the fever. Jeremiah was forced to restrict his girls to their own wagon. He was a focused man and his sustaining vision was to settle in Oregon near his brother. He would be able to own fertile land and build a farm. At least his daughters would live comfortably. At night he would relax by the fire and light his pipe and talk about the endless seashores of Oregon, the fragrant tall cedar trees, and the abundance of succulent wild berries begging to be picked. Their meager diet of bacon, beans and dry bread sorely lacked anything fresh, sweet, or juicy and the children dreamt of ripe plump blackberries.

In Laramie, a kind doctor treated the sick and they stocked up on supplies and fresh water. Within a week the journey continued and they trod the sand and baked clay of the Great American Desert. Maggie's friend Kathy, along with her parents and younger brothers, stayed behind. Kathy and her Mom had contacted cholera and were quarantined. She was not allowed to see her to say goodbye and she cried bitterly as Jeremiah ordered her into the wagon.

"You will see each other in Oregon," he assured Maggie although he was certain the woman and the child would not survive.

The desert alternated torments; unbearable heat during the day changed into bitter cold at night. Sometimes, though, the dry, brown clay gave way to sparse grassy surface sprouting prickly shrubs covered with small blossoms in vibrant colors. They saw herds of buffalo, an occasional antelope, and small animals that scurried across the dried ground and disappeared beneath clumps of sage. Tumbleweed would blow across the plain. It made great kindling for the evening fire but the girls had to be careful of its sharp painful pricks. Rosebud refused to chase the tumbleweed and cried in protest when urged by her father to help Maggie and Jenny.

Jeremiah thoroughly inspected the wagon and the gear each day to make sure everything was in working order. One morning he noticed a crack in the tongue. He pulled the wagon to the side and unyoked the oxen to begin the repair. Some of the other settlers offered assistance, but Jeremiah was certain he could take care of it himself and waved them on.

"Go on, we will catch up with you," he said, realizing that they would have to extend their traveling time during the day to make up for the lost hours. It took all morning to attach a brace giving the tongue the support necessary to eliminate further damage. The makeshift splint should hold until they reach their next settlement where, with the help of a blacksmith, a more permanent repair could be made.

A cloud of dust approached from the horizon as the children heard the thudding of a horse's hooves. Captain Morrow's Indian guide arrived in a veil of dust. He had been sent to check up on the Perrin family.

"We are fine, repairs are done."

Jeremiah offered him a cup of overbrewed coffee. The Indian gratefully accepted.

"We are hooking up the team and we will be right behind you."

The Indian waved and disappeared leaving a trail of red billowing clouds. Two o'clock in the afternoon and Jeremiah figured they had at least six hours of traveling time left before nightfall. The oxen started their slow trek covering two miles each hour. They were not the speediest team but reliable and good-natured and they never wandered off.

Evening was approaching and Jeremiah decided to make camp below a rocky slope that might provide lee against any night wind. Maggie and Jenny had been walking the trail, but Rosebud was sleeping in the wagon.

"Maggie get your sister out of the wagon."

He began to carefully lead the oxen down the incline. He saw tracks. The wagon train had created a smooth surface. The oxen struggled with their foothold and one of them slipped and the wagon started to slide. Jeremiah tried to keep the tilting, sliding wagon upright but was dragged underneath and crushed. The girls rushed to him but he did not move. Only his hair moved like wheat in a fall breeze; his blue eyes were lifeless. The oxen had clambered down the slope dragging the wagon that had fallen on its side. One wheel was broken.

* * *

The sun is slipping beneath a burnished sky. Maggie turns to her sisters.

"Let's get a fire going. Jenny you pick some brush."

Maggie appears calm and deliberate, her fears pushed aside. It could be months before another wagon train comes through. First, she thinks, they must eat and get some rest. She crawls into the wagon and searches for the old rusty coffeepot. She retrieves the bacon and bread and on her way back picks up her Papa's rifle. The girls settle on a blanket by the tumbleweed and deadwood fire Jenny had started. The fire and their closeness provide comforting warmth.

The desert is enveloped in darkness. Drifting clouds reveal occasional sparkling glitters in the night sky but the daytime breeze has died. The silence is fearful. Jenny moves closer to Maggie.

"I'm scared. I don't remember it ever being so quiet."

Maggie nods in silence. She struggles with the uncertainty of their future and tries to hide her fear. She must gather all of her strength, appear calm and set an example. Swallowing hard, she maintains a steady, even tone.

"There is nothing to be scared about. You have gotten used to the noise of the wagon train. That's all. Let's get some sleep."

She picks up the sleeping Rosebud. Rosebud's little round face is serene, the corners of her heart-shaped mouth curve up slightly. Maggie kisses her forehead and fervently prays that Rosebud is having happy dreams.

They climb into the wagon; it wobbles precariously, but settles. The oxen, having eaten and been given water, are resting nearby. The fire tumbles into small glowing embers as the girls' exhausted bodies surrender to sound sleep. Maggie, sleeping upright, leans her head against the rifle crooked inside her elbow.

Hours later, the wagon moans in protest as the oxen prod the canvas cover. Maggie wakes up in a flash of confusion and alarm. Her eyes open wide as reality slaps her as hard as the first light of the desert sun. She pulls herself together. She calls to Jenny awakening Rosebud who begins asking for Papa.

"Papa has gone to heaven. He is with Mamma now." Maggie lifts her little sister out of the wagon. Jenny is already searching for kindling.

"Maggie, there is no kindling; all the tumbleweed has blown away. There is only buffalo dung."

"Gather it. It burns just the same."

"You pick it up, Maggie; it smells so bad I want to faint." Jenny holds her nose with two fingers.

"Jen, don't be a baby. Pick the old, dried pieces—they'll burn better. Get going, we don't have time to waste."

Maggie searches through the wagon and picks food, a few tools, and pieces of clothing they must have as they continue the journey on foot. Her hands lovingly caress Mamma's hope chest that was to be hers. She touches the wooden clock that chimed, for as far back as she can remember, from the mantle over the fireplace at their home in Missouri. The expensive walnut and brass clock was a part of their past and was to be displayed proudly in their new homestead.

She scrambles out of the wagon carrying two canvas bags she straps to one of the oxen and then joins her sisters for breakfast. There is nothing new in their meal. She cuts Rosebud's bacon and breaks the dry hard bread into pieces she moistens by dunking into the coffee.

The sun's bright rays light up the desert. It is time to go. They pack up their food supplies and water canteen and strap them to the second ox. Maggie takes Rosebud's hand and, together with Jenny, they walk to the lonely grave and say goodbye to their father for the last time.

"Ho!"

Maggie snaps the rope to signal the oxen. Relieved of the heavy burden of the wagon, they immediately start the trek with a faster pace than before. There has not been any rain since the wagontrain left them behind and its tracks are clear. Rosebud bravely walks next to her big sister. Maggie has now become mother and father for her. Without hesitation, she puts her trust in her fourteen-year-old sister.

Jenny follows. She glances back at the battered wagon, the cold fireside and their father's grave. Tears swell in her eyes and she blinks them away when she sees Maggie's straight back in front of her. Maggie matches the oxen's determined pace, her brown curly hair fluttering beneath the bonnet. She turns and smiles reassuringly at Jenny. Her lips are tightly pressed together.

"Maggie, I'm tired," Rosebud says as she stumbles. Maggie lifts Rosebud onto the first ox, but as Rosebud falls asleep, she starts to slide and Maggie is forced to carry her little sister. The terrain slowly changes to a rough grassy plain. They approach a small group of oddly shaped trees. Maggie picks a tree and, under its shade, starts to prepare camp for the night. Papa would have been able to name the tree specimen. He identified the plant life along the way and encouraged the girls to discover new varieties. They had picked flowers for Momma who loved to smell their wonderful fragrance as she rested in the hot wagon.

The chatter of her bustling sisters rouses Maggie, drowsing against the trunk of the tree. There is ample kindling as well as feed for the oxen. They eat their dull and meager supper. Rosebud drifts off before she can finish her food and Maggie and Jenny soon fall into a deep dreamless sleep as well.

They awaken abruptly to a hard pelting rain. They cluster closely together with the sleeping Rosebud in their middle and wrap the blankets tightly around themselves. The tree gives some protection from the rain but when the gray, leaden dawn finally and slowly arrives, they are drenched. Shivering, they eat their bacon and bread. They have to forego the hot coffee as the area around them has turned into a muddy field with the steady rain and there is nothing dry enough to burn.

They pack up and move on. Maggie's bonnet is drooping around her ears and continuous streamlets slither down her back. Jenny's hat is pulled far down into her face as she follows the oxen. The girls are soaked to their bloomers and yearn for dry clothes and warm sunshine. The sun remains hidden behind the stormy gray clouds trudging across the monotone sky.

Near noon they reach what was probably a dry gully the day before but is now a raging stream. Maggie inspects the foaming muddy waters rushing by. Churning with deadwood and brush, this current will make a dangerous crossing.

"Jenny, you hold Rosebud's hand and don't let go. I am going to lead the first ox across then come back to get both of you."

Maggie pulls the lead rope and wades into the brown, rushing water. She is almost swept under as the animal frantically secures his footing and thrusts through the powerful current. The water reaches up to Maggie's chest. Safely across, she slowly starts back through the sweeping flood. She slips and disappears. To Jenny's relief, Maggie's head reappears and she sputters and spits the chocolate water. Her bonnet, however, rides the surge downstream at great speed. Maggie drags herself out of the water on her hands and knees.

"Jenny, the water is rising by the minute. We must cross now and use the other ox as support."

She ties the screaming Rosebud on top of the ox.

"Maggie, I'm scared." Jenny starts to shake. "I am not going into that water. I can't swim; you know that."

"Jenny, the water reaches up to my chest which means it's still not above your neck. You hold on to me as wade behind the ox." Maggie pushes the resisting animal into the water. Jenny has a firm grip on the ox's harness and Maggie has taken hold of the animal's coarse tail. Slowly, the ox pulls them forward.

A heavy broken limb smashes into the frightened animal's rump. The animal briefly stumbles and submerges. Jenny loses her grip and tumbles downstream, flailing the water. The ox resurfaces pushing desperately ahead and clambers up the bank. Maggie fights the muddy flow toward the bank as she shouts Jenny's name over and over. She can no longer see any sign of her sister across the roaring water. Jenny has been swept away without a trace.

She crawls up the muddy embankment. Jenny is gone. Across the raging waters, there is no bonnet, no dress, no ribbon. She staggers down along the ever-widening gully filled by the angry stream. The pounding rain blinds her and pelts her bruised body. Jenny is gone. Maggie falls on her knees. She hugs herself and lets out a desperate howl that is drowned in the roar of the stream and the downpour. Maggie crumbles and drops her face into her lap. She cannot bear still another loss.

"Maggie, help me!"

She raises her tear-streaked face. The ox with Rosebud still tied to his back is standing at her side. Rosebud is safe and tries to escape the confining ropes, uttering loud intermittent sobs. Rosebud—she almost forgot about her. Quickly, she jumps up and unties her. The child's face is scratched and bleeding and she complains of her tummy hurting where the ropes cut and bruised her skin. Maggie enfolds her small body and holds it tightly to her as she buries her face in the child's mudcaked curls.

"Where is Jenny?" Rosebud clings to her sister.

"She is with Mamma and Papa now," Maggie whispers.

They move on and Maggie searches the area. They must find some kind of shelter or they will surely die. Maggie carries Rosebud; the oxen follow. There is a dark clump ahead, barely visible through the shadowy curtain of rain. As they get closer, Maggie can make out a cluster of brush surrounding three small trees that will give them some protection. She cuts several branches of a broad-leaved tree and weaves them into the small bushes. She takes the sodden blanket and, pulling Rosebud behind her, crawls inside the primitive lean-to. She holds Rosebud closely to her as she rubs her sister's arms and legs. They nibble on soggy bread and she collects rainwater in the dented coffee cup.

Maggie's night is endless. Each time she closes her eyes Jenny's smiling face haunts her. She shouldn't have crossed the stream. Perhaps she could have tied Jenny to the ox like she did with Rosebud. She failed her sister. Why did Papa have to leave them? He would have delivered Jenny safely across the stream. He always said they are a family and must look out for each other. *When he wanted to teach the girls how to swim in the frog pond on their farm, Maggie had fun and learned quickly. Jen was very much afraid. She hated the water and ran into the house. Now, terribly, she is buried in a watery grave.

A silence intrudes. It stops raining. At dawn, the sun appears and lights up the prairie. It takes only a few hours for the mud to turn into clay baking once more into cracked patterns. Maggie spreads their clothes across the low-lying bushes and the girls sit wrapped in soggy blankets eating some dried beans.

Rosebud has stopped asking about Jenny. When the sun reaches mid-day overhead, they put on their dry clothes and start walking. It is hot and there is no shade but Maggie feels revived and more determined than ever to save her remaining sister.

The muted rumble of galloping horses prompts Maggie to shade her eyes and squint into the harsh afternoon sunlight. She spies two riders ahead, approaching at great speed. At first, Maggie thinks of the hostile Indians but then she recognizes the quickly approaching men. Captain Morrow and the Indian guide rein up their horses in a shower of baked mud.

"Girls, what happened to you?"

Captain Morrow dismounts and his tanned face is creased with concern.

"We figured that you should have caught up with us by now. Where are your Dad and sister?"

He glances quickly beyond the oxen.

Maggie opens her mouth to speak, but no sound emerges. Finally, she almost whispers, "They're gone!" Unbidden tears roll down her cheeks but she does not cry aloud. Captain Morrow puts his arm around her.

"Hush—you can tell us later. This is brutal country, but you and your sister are alive and that is what matters."

He lifts up Rosebud who is eyeing him fearfully. He hands her to the mounted Indian guide. Without fuss, she allows the Indian to place her in front of him and she wraps her tiny hands tightly around the pommel; riding with the Indian will be an exciting adventure.

"Come on girl," Captain Morrow takes Maggie by the hand, mounts his horse and pulls her up behind him. "You are going to be all right."

"Our oxen! They saved our lives!"

"Oh, they will catch up with us shortly." Captain Morrow gives her a big smile, "They have no wagon to pull or load to carry and they will follow our trail."

He turns to Rosebud. "You need some of Mrs. Sweeney's home cooking. When I last saw her she was fixing her famous stone soup full of the tasty meat of the antelope her husband shot this morning."

Rosebud looks at him curiously. She never had stone soup before. Her stomach starts to rumble. The Indian guide gives his horse a slight kick and it gallops off, following Captain Morrow and Maggie. Rosebud shrieks in delight. Maggie turns and smiles at her little sister and she knows that somehow, the two remaining Perrin homesteaders will realize her father's dream.

Journeys can be filled with peril as Maggie discovered. Sometimes, the peril is not a swollen stream, a rutted trail, or wild animals in an untamed land. Danger derived from laws of nature can be just as life-threatening when the law of nature you're fighting is the one that wants to keep you firmly anchored to mother earth—the law of gravity.

In the next tale, a great day for flying may turn out to be the <u>last</u> day for flying.

IT'S A GREAT DAY FOR FLYING

by

K. Kellogg Smith

I knew I was in trouble when the hot black oil spewed out of my plane's engine. Blown backwards by the slipstream, it put a thick coat of slick black oil on the windshield before it streamed back over the sleek yellow fuselage, making its way in thin streaks towards the tail.

Hitting the controls, dipping a wing, I could see black streaks of oil inching their way over the fuselage, could see them heading towards the electronics bay.

Can't let that oil get in there. Can't let it get to the plane's electronics.

Despite the loss of oil, the engine still sounded strong, running hard, the prop a nearly invisible blur. I hit the controls again, dropping the other wing to start a quick turn to the right. The landing field was down below. There were other planes circling the field, but the grass runway was clear.

Throttling my engine back to just above idle speed, both to reduce speed and to save my engine, I dipped the wings and signaled that I was declaring an emergency. The other aircraft in the pattern started clearing the area, going wide to give me a clear shot at the field.

I eased up on the controls to complete the right turn and straightened out, putting my plane on its base leg. But now my engine was beginning to pop, to stutter. Power was dropping. One more gliding right turn and I'd have the plane on final approach, the runway in sight. Just a few more moments and the plane would be safely on the ground.

"Don't give up on me now, baby ... don't give up on me now!" I breathed, easing the stick to put my plane into a slight, slipping right turn, lining up on the runway below.

The engine quit.

Instantly, I put the nose down a little, keeping up speed. Can't afford to stall now!

I hit the switch to drop the landing gear. The gear doors popped open like they were supposed to. I could almost hear the electric motors whining as the landing gear dropped and locked into place, rubber tires spinning.

My plane glided the last few yards and crossed safely over the rutted dirt road at the end of the field. A light touch on the controls. Nose up slightly now, let her stall. Good baby! Touchdown! A slight bouncing run, wings wobbling. A bit of right rudder to turn her as she slowly came to a stop, nose pointing towards the flight line.

"Nice landing, Grampa!" Ryan laughed, clapping his hands together. "I thought you were going to lose it when the engine quit like that."

I laughed, ran my hand through his honey-blond hair.

"Naw, Ryan. Not an old pilot like me," I laughed. "Been flying these things too long for that!"

I put the radio control transmitter down, flag-tipped antenna pointing out toward the field. The field controller gave Ryan and me an okay to go out and get our plane, its sleek yellow wings and fuselage glinting in the afternoon sun.

"It's a great day for flying model airplanes, isn't it, Ryan."

"It sure is, Grampa. It sure is!"

We now move from the dangers of an oil slick to the dangers of an ice slick. In the true stories that follow, Lu Maistros relates anecdotes from the icy patches of her childhood in the far north of upper Vermont.

In a time before seatbelts were legislated and when airbags only referred to pompous uncles, families resorted to winter driving techniques that would give Ralph Nader a heart attack.

Here's a healthy helping of the cold with a dash of the hope of spring.

GROWING UP COLD:
A MEMOIR OF GROWING UP COLD, BUT LONGING TO BE COOL, IN 1950'S VERMONT
(An excerpt reprinted by permission of PublishAmerica)

by

Lucille Maurice Maistros

JANUARY

Dad's Cold War – assault on a high ground

It was clear that my parents had not bought our house in the winter, clinging as it was to the side of Mountain Avenue, a street so steep that, even in summer, men came from all over to test their brakes driving down our street. Then they would turn their cars around at the bottom and drive back up again, their tires spitting sand and gravel from under the fenders. We could have sold bumper stickers, like the ones for Mount Washington: *this car climbed Mountain Avenue*.

Winter was inconvenient at best, dangerous at worst. In a place so dominated by the weather, every month brought with it new challenges, but ironically, what challenged and frustrated us also provided entertainment.

We learned at a young age not to dawdle under the eaves where icicles dangled menacingly from the edges of the roof. They would drip and grow longer during the January thaw, then freeze again into icy skirts that brushed the tops of the snow banks all around the house. And despite a day or two of warming in January, the snow would just keep coming. And coming. You could shovel every day, as we did, lifting and heaving huge shovelsfull onto the sides of the driveway, unti l the driveway was a car-sized luge—the surface never entirely snow-free and the walls iced-over canyons.

When it came to the challenges of Mountain Avenue, my father was no different than other men, if anything even more determined to get his car in our driveway, no matter what. One afternoon, the first winter Dad had the 1959 Chrysler Windsor with the tailfins, my brothers and I stood waiting for him to come home. It was dusk, about 4 o'clock. We were finished shoveling, cold and tired, and supper was almost ready, but we had to watch Dad come home.

As any Vermonter will tell you, there is an art to driving uphill in the winter: if you apply too much gas, your tires will spin and you won't go anywhere. Any hesitation, however, and your car will sense it, like a willful mule, and the rear end will balk, smacking into anything around it. It takes experience. It takes a standard shift. And it takes a determined man like my father. Although the Chrysler was an automatic, Dad knew how to tease the transmission from *Low* to *Drive*. In the age before SUVs, he was a man who could drive *any* car *any* place.

On this particular day, though, he wasn't having any luck. It had been snowing since he left for work that morning and the street under the new fallen snow was slick. Crawling through powder up over the tires, the car swam all over the place, once or twice just missing the stone wall under the lilac bushes. Finally, he stopped at the bottom of the hill, climbed out of the car and opened the trunk. He stood there for a minute, in those big black rubber galoshes unbuckled over his work shoes, a red plaid wool jacket, and a gray, billed cap pulled low over his forehead, pondered for a minute or two, hands on hips, and then motioned for us to come down. We ran. "Sit in the trunk," he ordered when we slid to a stop, "put some weight on those rear tires." Then he settled himself back in behind the wheel.

You couldn't do anything in this neighborhood without attracting a crowd. In a moment, a half-dozen other kids had climbed into the trunk with us. Most of them were Ducharmes who lived next door to us and, with fourteen kids, were the largest Catholic family in Scotia County. Today, using kids as trunk ballast would elicit a barrage of editorials and horrified letters asking what kind of man would risk children's lives this way. But this was a time when everyone smoked, ate fried food and drove without seatbelts. We didn't know any better.

After we were all settled in the open trunk, our legs dangling between the tailfins like an octopus rear-ending a killer whale, Dad slammed the car door and revved up those 450 horses for one last go. The Madonna on the dashboard trembled as the Chrysler started to lumber up the street, now as sure-footed as a Sherman tank. He kept his foot on the gas and we were moving so fast when he hit the driveway that we almost overshot the end of it—he hit the brakes before we mowed down the stand of pine trees just beyond.

The smell of burning rubber. The whine of spinning tires. Winter didn't get much better than this.

The rites of spring

It is hard to believe, standing in a snowdrift in mid-January, that spring will ever come to the Northeast Kingdom. But one day you're shoveling another snowstorm from the yard; the next, it seems, you're picking yellow dandelions from the lawn while a wave of melting snow sends a foaming wall of water plowing down the Oompassaic River.

Springtime is rhubarb time. Rhubarb is a bitter vegetable, but in Vermont, after a long gray winter, people tend to grab any green shoot no matter how unpalatable, and cook it. Rhubarb. Dandelion greens. Once when I was four, I pulled a fistful of tiger lily shoots out of the ground and ate them, thinking they were string beans. I've forgotten what they tasted like but they couldn't have been any worse than unsweetened rhubarb. In the case of rhubarb, all it took was a pound or two of sugar and Mom could make delicious, sweet-tart rhubarb pie and rhubarb sauce.

Leave it to Vermonters to take this time of year, which combines the dreariness of winter and the cheerless experience of mud season, and make a game out of it. The people of the village of Indian Pond have a contest that has shown to be a more accurate predictor of spring than that rodent in Pennsylvania. They hold a year-long lottery as to what date and time the ice on the pond will melt. Anyone can submit a guess at the Indian Pond General Store. Tourists who stop in for postcards and maple syrup are intrigued and will take a moment to jot down their guesses and drop them into a mason jar on the counter, next to the home-baked bread and brownies heaped by the cash register. Leon Smith, the owner of the store as well as the postmaster of the village of Indian Pond, lives on the lake year round and is in charge of determining when the exact time occurs. He ties a cord to a cinder block and puts it on a wooden pallet on the frozen lake behind his cottage. Then he ties the other end to an electric clock on the back porch. When the ice melts, the cinder block plunges into the lake or floats away on the wood, but either way, the clock is unplugged. As long as records have been kept, the earliest that the ice has melted was on April 18, the latest on May 6.

The actual first sign of spring, when I was a kid, was when our mothers finally let us take off some of our woolies for the walk to school. We were suddenly weightless, like that trick, you know, where you push your arms real hard up against a doorframe and when you step out your arms just float up on their own? What a relief after carrying around all that extra padding since November. What a relief to leave it all in the closet. Ski pants, parkas, boots, scarves, earmuffs, gloves. Our eyes, no longer shaded by hoods and scarves, blinked at the new spring sun. For the first time since Thanksgiving, we could see and hear where we were going.

I, personally, was anxious to strip off the ugly cotton-knit tights—supposedly flesh-colored but only in the way that an ace bandage is flesh-colored—that my mother insisted I wear to keep my legs warm under my uniform. As the air grew warmer, it brought with it a renewed hope that this year I would finally be *cool*.

Certainly, the cold of northern New England is chilling to the bone but nowhere as cold as those dead and dying on the battlefield. Charlotte R. Wrublewski takes us back nearly six hundred years in a slice of historical fiction to the very real and very cold twilight on the fields of Grunwald. Her images of this historic fight between two medieval powers is a chilling reminder of the savagery of war and the consequences for the survivors.

SEARCHERS IN THE MIST

by

Charlotte R. Wrublewski

CHAPTER ONE
THE FIELD

The men lay where they had been slain, some contorted and some at peace as in slumber. Like other battles that had gone before it was the women who came to claim their men. That hot July summer's day grew colder with death on the ground absorbing the congealing blood of the fallen and dismembered. The year of our Lord 1410. The battlefield was Grunwald where the Black Knights of Poland met the Teutonic Knights of Germany.

The adversaries both bore the Christian cross on their chests. The Teutonic knights wore white tunics and white helmets with masks that covered their faces, and the crimson cross across their chests.

Christians fought against Christians. The battle lasted more than ten hours. Hand to hand, knight against knight, they fought with axes, lances, swords and maces. The Polish noble classes of knights were pitted against the powerful Teutonic knights.

The Black Knights of Poland wore black tunics and black helmets with masks that covered their faces, and an ever-present crimson cross on their chests. When they first appeared in battle, the Poles presented a fearsome sight. Like the masked black falcons they trained, their potential looked ominous. Clothed entirely in black, with only the red cross on their chests, they looked like marble chess pieces and invincible to those who saw them on the hill overlooking the battlefield.

The Teutonic knights, clothed and helmeted in white, contrasted sharply with the Black Knights. Clean and benign in their white uniforms, they looked angelic—a look that belied their undeniable strength and ruthlessness.

German knights had a singular and focused mind. It was they who had turned the pagan populations of northern Europe into Christians by their swords and brutality that spared no one. They came to destroy the last vestiges of their opponents' primitive beliefs.

The Germans had defeated the Poles prior to this meeting. But this battle had to be the turning point for the Polish kingdom; this conflict was desperate and pivotal. If the Poles lost, their existence as a culture would be in doubt. Germans had the potential to swiftly overrun Polish lands and subjugate all inhabitants. There was much for the Poles to loose.

When the battle was over, the Poles had decisively won. What was the cost? Bodies of both Teutonic knights and Polish knights were crushed, hacked to pieces and pierced. Where the axes had struck men they were decapitated or disemboweled. By the force of two-handed swords, some men were cut in half.

Women who came to the battlefield watched the crimson sun go down in the west. What remained was a scene of settling dust, diminishing heat and a rising fog that clouded this lower rim of earth. The silence was palpable and significant. The women brought their priests to give the last rites of the Church for both friend and enemy.

Angela, the young mistress of her family's estate, came looking for her brother Janusz. Anxious at not seeing him immediately and shocked by the slaughter, her heart began to pound and the pulse in her throat began to beat a heightened rhythm. Her thoughts focused on her young brother. Before the battle had begun he had set forth proudly to meet the foe. His horse, Kostanek, which meant Chestnut, was now nowhere to be seen.

In the distance some low moans could be heard as the women advanced seeking their fallen men. Sobs were heard when some of the women came upon their fallen kin. The men who were still alive heard the women and began faint bodily movements in the hope of being saved.

The victors returned from the far reaches of the battlefield to survey what could be done. Peter of Torun, the tall leader of the

Black Knights, called to his men to carefully search the vast field for survivors.

Angela, her face stricken with concern and horror and covered with a layer of dust from the battlefield, called to him, "What of Janusz my brother? What has become of him? Do you know?"

"Have you seen Janusz?" she called once again. "Perhaps he's back at the castle in Torun, by some chance?" She beseeched him with tears brimming in her soft green eyes.

Peter lifted the beaver of his helmet and, recognizing the tall fair-haired young woman who in her grief blended in with the bedraggled group of women, said, "He's not back at the castle in Torun, and his vassal cannot be found either."

At this Angela groaned and spoke in a barely audible voice.

"Thank you, sir. We'll continue to look. If we could have more lanterns when darkness falls, we will be able to continue our search."

"We'll return with more help, my lady," he responded, and galloped south to Torun with some of his men.

Angela and her much younger brother, Pavel, stumbled and stepped over the dead to where there were some sounds in a remote field close to the forest. In order to make their way, they had to step aside the piles of bodies of men and dead horses. The smell of blood and gore began to overcome her and she quickly tied her handkerchief around her nose. The acrid odor of soon-to-be-decaying flesh was too much for her fourteen-year-old brother, Pavel.

"I can't bear this, Angela! Let's go back!" he cried.

"Wait, I'll tear some of my skirt and you can use it to cover your face."

She ripped apart some of the lace of her skirt, and tied a makeshift mask for Pavel.

"Here, this will help."

By now tears were streaming down Pavel's dusty face. Rivulets coursed down his cheeks and onto his shirt. His long-held scapular was beginning to fray around his neck from the struggle of the day and the heat.

Angela realized that the grief and strain of the potential loss of her older brother had profoundly affected Pavel and diminished his self-control. Words of comfort that ordinarily were a part of her nature could not rise from her heart to her lips. But there was still some hope. It was difficult to find the right words.

"Let's move on," she said. "I see some horses moving at the edge of the woods…Janusz may be there."

The knights, in their rush to gather help for the few survivors of the battle, had not rounded up the horses that had survived the clash. Horses slowly began to come out of the woods and, facing the battlefield, they began to turn their attention to their fallen masters. From hope of water or merely from fatigue, they halted themselves despite no orders to do so.

Night fell and the world seemed to grow more horrible yet. A large group of peasants appeared with lanterns and lit fagots to illuminate the darkened battlefield.

CHAPTER TWO
THE FOREST GIVES UP ITS PRIZE

The peasants joined Angela and Pavel in their search for Janusz. Their fires and lanterns lit up the field and the edge of the forest. The grounds were strewn with broken lances and shields. The peasants found the horses near the woods.

"Aha, look, these warriors too are lost and confused," they cried.

"It's Kostanek!" cried Pavel as he saw one horse covered with dirt and blood. Kostanek neighed and stamped his right front hoof, but did not run. The saddle was torn and hung down from his left flank. A shield was riven and chipped on the ground beside him.

The peasants ran closer to the horse and stopped abruptly as they saw a knight's body.

"Janusz!" Angela cried at seeing him.

When they reached him they saw that his arm had been partially severed. Blood covered his tunic so that the crimson of the cross mingled with the blood seeping from his wound.

Janusz was barely conscious from his loss of blood. His vassal, Marcus, was dead by his side with the stump of a lance protruding from his chest.

Rana, a peasant maid, ran swiftly to Janusz's side. She knelt beside him, and quickly put her hand to his nose to feel for for breath with her sun-tanned hand. Her coal-black hair had fallen from her kerchief and covered her face as she ministered to him.

"He is still alive," she cried to the gathering crowd.

"Oh, Mother of God, please save Janusz," Angela pleaded softly as she and the peasant women attempted to free his clothes from the constraints of his armor and to staunch the blood seeping from his arm with some makeshift bandages they had made from shredded garments.

Rana, gently lifting Janusz's blood-soaked head, brought some mead to Janusz's lips and said, "Take small sips."

Only a faint movement of his head acknowledged that there was life in his body.

"Janusz, Janusz, God has saved you!" Angela cried.

Peasants and the newly-arrived knights were heartened at seeing him alive. They quickly began to make a stretcher for their fallen comrade to take him back to the castle.

With his sister and young brother by his side, the tattered and torn knight was carried back to the castle at Torun. The Polish knights had been garrisoned at the castle with their horses, armor and arms gathered there in preparation for the battle at Grunwald.

When they arrived at the castle they gently placed Janusz on a makeshift table in the Great Hall where Peter of Torun, the chief of the Black Knights, attempted to assess his wounds.

"His arm will have to be cut away," he said, "there is no method by which we can save it."

The surgeon was called and quickly agreed with Peter's assessment. As the surgeon's apprentices made Janusz ready, Peter called for the priest to come and give the last rites of the Church. Seeing the priest, Friar Thomas, Angela fell on her knees and beseeched him, "Ask God to save my brother, please!"

The surgery was brief but painful. His arm had already been partially severed by the German's sword. It had to be amputated where it had been slashed. Blood was staunched by the skill of the surgeon where he expertly cauterized veins and arteries. The surgeon did his job well.

"He'll need good care now," the surgeon advised Angela. "The rest is in the hands of the Almighty, and by the care and love of you, his sister," he added.

If he survived his loss of blood the knight might live. Janusz was young and this would be in his favor. He had been strong and athletic before he was struck. His prospect of going to war had created joy within his heart; his spirit was strong. He never questioned his own courage. It had been a clear duty for him to ride into battle. It was an honor for him to follow Peter of Torun and his fellow knights. He knew what might happen and accepted it without a murmur and without thought of consequences.

For his younger brother Pavel, who had become overwrought with grief and despair at the sights and aftermath of the bloody battlefield at Grunwald, a growing rage at the consequences of war itself began to fester in his heart.

"When will all these wars be over?" he cried, addressing his anguish to Peter.

"We may never know, but our future will be peace for many years after this. Be assured," Peter responded.

His own face was reddened from the sun and the intensity of the battle. His dark brown hair was now matted with his sweat and dust from the earth. Seeing Janusz near death and the loss of so many men instilled within him a resolve that something better had to happen for his people and those men who went out to wage this battle.

"We have won, after all. The Germans have surrendered," Peter said.

The love Pavel and Angela have for Janusz may be far removed from our time but love and love's memories are timeless.

In "Orange Crush," our next selection, the memories of love are evoked by nothing more than the citrus tang of a soft drink flavor. At least, Lois Gilbert remembers it as a first love. Perhaps it was only a crush.

ORANGE CRUSH

by

Lois Gilbert

She took a sip. The pungent orange flavor made her mouth pucker. An Orange Crush. It had been her favorite drink, way back when. She could not believe that her sister had remembered. Why, she had even apologized when she couldn't find it in the old-fashioned, dark brown bottles. Her sister had given her this six-pack on this, her sixtieth birthday.

She stepped out on the deck and took another sip. Clark's Filling station. Clark's, a dusty white cinder block building with slope-shouldered old pumps and a thriving drive-in food service, had been just over the bridge that crossed the Tar River outside of the small town in eastern North Carolina where she had grown up. In the forties, Clark's was the place to be after a date at the movies.

The squat station sat in the middle of a large concrete parking lot. The back of the lot was bordered with pine trees and an unidentifiable thicket as tangled as her sister's morning hair. The lights from the station were only a glow under the pines. It was the favorite place to park after the movies. An Orange Crush at Clark's. They brought it on a tray they hung on the window. She couldn't remember the movie they had seen but she would never forget that the car radio had been playing "Night and Day."

The telephone rang; she didn't answer. Lost in reverie, she took another sip. She remembered Murray's lips. She and Murray were sixteen and so in love. Murray gave her her first kiss under the pines. His lips felt chapped. Were they supposed to feel like that? Had hers felt the same? The tingle of an Orange Crush remained. Thank goodness.

She looked out across the fields. There were no pines. She heard the door slide open behind her. "What's up?" he asked.

She felt his arms move around her. She turned her head and felt his lips on hers. Why, <u>his</u> lips weren't chapped at all.

"Want a sip?"

Joe took the bottle from her.

The memories of a first love and a first kiss may be sweet for Lois Gilbert, but the memory of love is framed in deep blue for the policeman protagonist in the next story. His job is certainly dangerous and a policeman's life can be cut short in the time it takes a bullet to get from barrel to brain. Tom was always ready for the bullets but was blindsided by his wife's bout with cancer. Losing his wife was a blow difficult enough to endure but the potential loss of his daughter as well sends him...well...off balance.

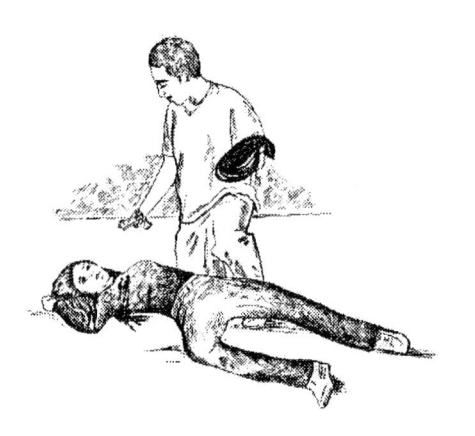

BALANCE

by

Ted M. Zurinsky

When the phone rang, the bomb went off. Not much of a bomb, really, but it got my attention. Phil Betterman, my heavy-set, burrito-addicted friend from our bomb squad, said the C4 involved couldn't have been much more powerful than a cherry bomb or half an M80.
"Tom," he mused between bites, "This bomber's either very good or very bad." CSI had already cleared my daughter's bedroom and they were cleaning up in the rest of the house. They had nothing so far. Phil was picking through what remained of my daughter's phone on the blackened night table. He looked back at me while holding up what now looked like a charred mobile from hell's ceiling. "Who've you pissed off who's either an expert or a klutz with C4?"
I shrugged but I knew exactly who, of course.
"You know," he said turning his attention to one last bean on the Taco Bell wrapper, "Martina would have been hurt but almost certainly would have survived. I'd think it was some rejected ninth grade geek with access to internet bomb making know-how except it's C4, not blackpowder. Where would a kid get C4? And a kid might have intended to hurt without killing. If it's one of your convicted and paroled hardcases, maybe it's a warning of some kind. But then, why Martina's phone instead of your phone in the bedroom?"
I shook my head and headed back to the living room couch. I shook my head, not because I didn't understand the warning, but because I still wanted to deny the balance, the symmetry of the attack.
Life on a seesaw. In the morning I was almost happy. My high school sophomore daughter, Martina, had headed off to the mall with some older girlfriends and I was whistling and picking

up some clothes in her bedroom. I remember the phone rang once and I started for it. The next thing I knew, I was sitting on my ass with my ears ringing and smoke curling around the ceiling. The explosion itself may not have knocked me down; the shock may have been enough. The EMT's checked me out and wanted me to go to the hospital but I declined. I felt okay and I wanted to be here when Martina returned. Ever since her mother died, Martina's been my only reason to keep on. Now, Robert J. Winthrop, Jr., was telling me I wouldn't have her for long. Life on a seesaw.

Three years ago, life seemed perfect. Mary and I had been married for fifteen years ten of which we spent constantly renovating this old farmhouse in which Martina and I now bounce around like pinballs. Martina was a wonderfully sports-driven, carefree, strawberry-blond, freckled, pizza-munching middle schooler with only a vague awareness of boys. Mary was a blue-eyed country girl-become-woman who tended our large garden, weeded out our adolescent's problems, and planted in me the greatest contentment while I tried to solve murders as one of our city's finest homicide detectives. Then came the lump, diagnosis, surgery, radiation, chemo, wasting, cutting of the biggest part of my heart, anger, grief, and aimlessness. The ragged-toothed saw end of the seesaw.

After a couple of months, I realized Mary would never forgive me if I didn't give Martina a chance to soften the memories and grow into the woman Mary would've loved and admired. So I pretended to be okay and that helped Martina. After a while, I began to be okay—at least enough to watch Martina become a high-school math whiz, develop an interest in somebody named Bill...and, simultaneously, another somebody named Shawn...and move to first string sweeper on the soccer team. Then came the night I had just picked up milk and bread on the way home from the precinct and was the closest unit to a silent alarm trip at Unburied Treasures, a fine jewelry shop on the edge of the city.

When I pulled into the alley next to the shop with my lights out, the front door looked secure and no windows were broken. I got out and checked the steel sidedoor. The spring bolt had been taped back and the door was slightly ajar. Someone had deftly rewired the outside alarm but I knew a lot of these stores had redundancy in the use of motion sensors inside. The thief thought he had all the time in the world and didn't know three more units were silently speeding here. I drew my Smith and Wesson 9mm and a penlight and stepped inside.

"Police! Police! Put your hands up and step forward to my light!"

Dark and silent as a Roman catacomb.

Suddenly, three quick shots sparked out from the front of the shop, two zinging just above my right ear and the third breaking glass in the display cabinet to my left. I fired three rapid shots at the center of the muzzle blasts and, after a half second, heard a slight grunt and the thud of body and gun. I ran forward, kicked the gun away, and bent over the sprawled figure, camoed in black from shoes to hooded mask. I pulled off the hood and long black hair spilled out in a pool like inky blood. I felt her neck but there was no hint of a pulse. No wonder. I saw three crimson holes in her black pullover.

Afterwards, the shakes from adrenalin, shouting, lights, clearing the scene, a short stint of required counseling. Burglary also figured out the rest of the story. Wendy Winthrop was probably on her first job. We don't know whether she was trying to prove something to her master-thief husband or just trying to live life on the edge. She certainly didn't need the cash. Robert Winthrop, Jr., had inherited more than twenty-two million from his family and augmented it, we suspected, by widely-separated perfect heists in a tri-state area. We wouldn't have had a clue if we didn't get a tip from a snitch who supplied a piece of his equipment. Still, we could prove nothing in any of the cases.

On the night of Wendy's coming-out party, Robert was busy losing some hundreds at a poker party he hosted at his mansion. Some of the most prominent names in the county, including one judge, played that night and, after some low-key interviews, we determined Robert Winthrop couldn't have been involved. It's likely he never even knew.

He knew who I was, though. The press interviewed my captain and me in the squadroom after Wendy Winthrop was killed. They wanted to know about the shooting and if Wendy had pulled the other unsolved heists. I don't know how he got upstairs but Robert stood behind some reporters with his arms folded and both eyes boring into me as surely as the three bullets I had put into his wife. I flinched, not because I thought I had done anything wrong but because I recognized his anger at losing his wife more than he could ever know. A second later and he was gone.

Three months later came the phone bomb. An announcement more than a warning, really. Robert had worked with explosives in some of his burglaries and he had almost limitless resources and great skill. The size of the bomb was no mistake; he wanted me to know he was going to kill my daughter and he wanted me to suffer helplessness as well as her loss.

I tried to prepare. I put better locks on the doors, installed a good wireless alarm system, and insisted Martina never stay at home alone. I'd tail her at a distance to make sure she was okay when going to the mall or the movies with friends. But I knew I was kidding myself. Winthrop was an expert at B and E, had all the free time in the world, and was driven by hate as deep as my anxiety. I also had a job to do and couldn't watch Martina every minute of every day. His plan to make me suffer was working.

I stopped worrying after the night of Martina's homecoming dance. Martina had just gotten her driver's license and had wrung permission from me to drive our Nissan Pathfinder with Shawn (Bill had lost the competition for her attention, I guess), Sharon, and her date, Brian. While Martina primped, I had time on my hands. I walked outside and checked the woods with a set of infrared binoculars I bought. I walked the thirty paces to the garage and checked the dark recesses with a flashlight. I looked at the Pathfinder gleaming dark blue in the moonlight. I checked the doors—all locked. I opened the car, popped the hood and looked at the engine—all okay. I dropped to my knees and looked under the car and went cold. There, under the driver's seat, my flashlight revealed better than a pound of C4 with blasting cap wired to the ignition. Incredibly, all my fear disappeared to be replaced in an instant with a calm as placid as a flat pond. I slowly removed the cap, detached the C4, and ripped the wires from the ignition leads.

Sure, I followed her to the dance but I knew nothing would happen that night. Winthrop had somehow discovered Martina was going to drive the Pathfinder that night and would assume a wire had failed when he saw nothing in the news the next day. He'd merely wait for another opportunity.

The next day, I went to another city and bought a couple of cellphones under false names. I visited Phil Betterman's Bomb Squad office, swiped a few texts, and returned them secretly a few days later. I followed Robert Winthrop on my off time and learned his habits. Smoking, television news, card tricks, and gourmet cooking. And one obsessive habit. Although he drove several cars from his garage during the day, every night from eight to nine he'd joy drive his favorite: a classic Jaguar 3.8 liter sedan. It didn't have an alarm.

Last night, I found my chance. He dashed into a small, expensive market and I opened the car with a jimmy and put the package under his seat. I relocked the car and walked away.

Tonight, I'm in the alley outside Irish Eyes, the hangout for precinct cops, and we're having a retirement party for Harry Pannerd, a guy from Robbery Division. It's eight twenty-five. With the ocean of beer already consumed, everyone's feeling good and no one's noticed me duck out to the alley for a second.

You see, I just want a little balance, a little symmetry, a little peace and protection from the awful possibilities of fate and hate. So after I call, I'll smash the phone, stick it in a bag, and put it in the garbage bin—no prints, no loose ends, no explosive I ever bought. The police might figure he's a burglar who blew himself up by accident. The public might think, after his wife's death, that he killed himself. I know he's waiting to achieve his version of balance, waiting to become Martina's murderer.

When the phone rang, the bomb went off.

Whether or not you approve of Tom's solution to the threat posed to his daughter, you can understand his desperation to save her at all costs. But what of those terrible instances in which parents can do nothing to save a daughter? How do parents endure the holes in their souls? Perhaps when those stricken parents are forced to live through the terrible ordeal of a lost child and find themselves in the basement of despair, there still may be hope in the attic.

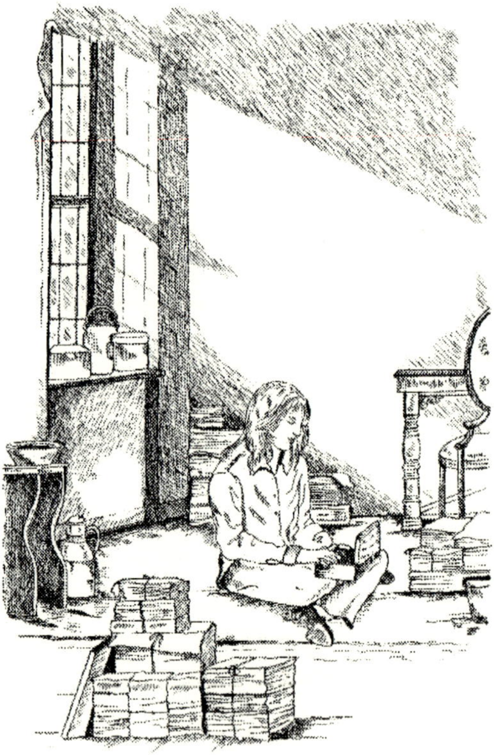

HOPE IN THE ATTIC

by

Mary Beth Creighton

Carefully peeling back the plastic bubble wrap, I looked down at the hand-carved teak box I had gotten at the beach souvenir shop when I was a teenager, my treasure box. Over eight years ago, when Charlie and I first moved into our old Victorian near the seaside cliffs, I had tucked it away in a remote corner of the attic and forgotten it.

Finding an empty spot among the stacks of cardboard, I sat cross-legged on the dusty floor and placed the box on my lap. I sat reminiscing in the attic for a very long time while the winter winds swirled outside, the cone of sunlight from the cracked dormer window a blanket of warmth in the chilled room.

Attics are supposed to be dark and foreboding, lairs of monsters and full of ominous creaks. Perversely, I was the kind of child for whom attics were places to explore, where adventures could be imagined and treasures found. I had become an adult; attics were places to avoid—mice skittered on rafters, dust clogged your lungs and boxes of junk were forgotten.

I only went up in our attic because we were considering selling, moving out, and—most traumatic of all—going our separate ways. Charlie was thinking southwest, I was thinking northeast. We were already more apart than that even though we lived in the same house.

We had become so good at pretending everything was normal. It was sad how politely we treated each other, how civil we were as we talked about where we might live and what we might do, deliberately avoiding discussing our daughter, what had become of us. At least we finally admitted it was time to part ways and leave our old house and all its memories.

It was a wonderful old house. Amber had loved roaming its nooks and spaces, often hiding in the back stairs or playing her flute in our little parlor. Framed in red mahogany molding with rosettes above the corners of the doorways, the room was always her favorite. She would sit by the parlor's French doors, the brick patio and gardens just beyond. I could still picture all her pretty dolls lined up on the chintz sofa to enjoy her concerts. Her music had filled the house with such joy, her joy.

She would be so sad that we were leaving the house, leaving it in separate directions.

I sighed, thinking about the task ahead of me, wondering why I was compelled to search the packages up in our attic. It would have been easier to avoid peeking in the boxes. We hadn't opened them in years. Why bother now when it would be more efficient just to take them straight to the dump? After all, I didn't keep Amber's things up here. I had packed them months ago in plastic containers, still sitting on her bed—her dolls, her cloths, her little white dress shoes with a pink flower on the buckles, her flute.

Every room in the house reminded me of Amber, her love for life and her radiating essence. Every room reminded me that she was gone.

Sadly, my husband might as well be gone. I had already lost him too. After several months of the chasm growing between us, my grief had turned into a kind of walking numbness.

Now I sat in the attic with my forgotten treasure box, mustering the courage to look inside because I knew it would be painful to see what Charlie and I had once been to each other.

One hinge was broken, and I nearly snapped off the lid when I opened the box to look inside. I already knew what I would find: the pressed petals of the first rose Charlie had ever given me, the love letters he had written me on the cash register receipts of the McDonalds he had worked at, the gumball machine ring he had bought me as a joke, the poems he had inspired me to write.

I hadn't expected the stab to my gut, the tightening in my chest. It was all there and I cried as I read my poems, read every word Charlie had written to me about getting married someday and starting a family, loving each other until we passed from one world to the next.

It all seemed so simple then, before bills and job demands, before being bone tired from working all night so our little girl didn't have to go to daycare, before we knew how scary the world was with murder and greed and fanaticism. Before our little girl died of lymphoma while we watched helplessly as she withered away despite all the doctors, the treatments, and the prayers. Before I drifted apart from the only man I had ever loved so passionately, so deeply.

My first slow tears became sobs and I didn't realize Charlie had found me there in the attic until I felt the warmth of his closeness, his large comforting hand on my shoulder. I quieted and he sat down next to me and read the poems, the letters, rubbed his thumb across the plastic ring.

"What's this?" he asked quietly, reaching under my rose petals to retrieve another folded piece of cellophane.

"Oh, our hair. Remember?" We had cut pieces of our hair just before we graduated form high school and given the locks to each other to take to college, Charlie having gone out of state for school, me staying in town at a local university. We'd put our locks together in my treasure box when we were reunited and married, just before we moved to the little apartment with the slanted kitchen floor, our first home together.

Smiling slightly, I unwrapped the plastic and was surprised to see not two, but three locks of hair. Nestled amongst one of Charlie's brown curls and my pin-straight strand was a braid of honey gold, Amber's hair before she lost it from the chemotherapy treatments.

I held it up to my nose to inhale her familiar scent, salty from the sea air. She felt so close. It was almost as if she were in the attic with us. Looking at Charlie, I lifted my brows in question. "I didn't know you had put this here."

"I didn't." He took the braid from my fingers, stroked it with his own. "I haven't been up here since we moved in, since before Amber was born."

"Me either," I murmured, tears spilling once more down my cheeks. "She wouldn't have come here alone, would she?"

"Maybe she wasn't alone...she's not alone now," Charlie suggested. Drawing in a deep breath, he gently put Amber's hair back with ours and carefully folded the cellophane. He gently brushed my tears with his knuckles. He took my hand, pressed it against his heart. "I've had such a hole in my heart since Amber died, since I lost you too."

Words failed me as he gathered up our treasures and put them into the box, tucked it under his arm and helped me to my feet.

"She'd want us to stay together," he said quietly, his warm walnut eyes serious and intent. "For all the right reasons."

"I have a hole too," I choked out, my voice quivering with emotion.

"Then let's start filling them up again."

"Oh Charlie!" I waited a beat then moved into his outstretched arms. We held each other for the first time in months finally beginning to share what we had buried away, our grief, our pain, and our love for one another.

As the fragments of the setting sun filtered through the cracked windowpane, we left the attic tentatively holding hands, the dust motes dancing around us like fairies. Whether we stayed in our old house or moved on, it would be together. I was suddenly sure of it; as sure as I was that our daughter would always be a part of our lives, guiding us, sustaining us until we were all three together once again.

Attics are full of treasures, treasures that are often full of memories, and memories that are often full of hope.

Amber's braid preserved a memory and, perhaps, even a marriage in "Hope in the Attic." We can, unfortunately, no more see beyond the scope of the story than we can imagine possessing a sense other than sight, smell, taste, touch, or hearing. We can imagine what life would be like not having one of our senses.

Put a blindfold on and you begin to feel what blindness is. Put a clothespin on your nose, have someone put a substance in your mouth, and you suddenly realize how much your sense of smell is the coach for your sense of taste. And what if the sounds of birds, music, and your own children's laughter were to disappear? What if your friends thought they were sharing fond memories with you and you couldn't hear them? Lois Gilbert shares her real life story of trying to recapture a precious sense.

HEARING...LOST AND FOUND

by

Lois Gilbert

I heard the rain as it pelted the roof. I heard the fan from the powder room. I could hear the TV that I had left on. Had these sounds been there yesterday? All but the rain. I closed the closet doors and started down the stairs. There was the hum of the refrigerator. Had I finally found a solution to a previously muted world?

I was a member of one of the last generations to have a mastoid operation. Penicillin was the cure for the infection many of us suffered. My parents were told that I would eventually have a hearing deficiency in my right ear; unfortunately, a correct diagnosis.

When attending meetings, I arrived early so I could find a spot close to the speaker. Our children teased me about the loudness of our TV. I didn't take that too seriously because Joe and I had teased his parents about the same thing. Then while on a visit to California to see our son, he asked, "Mom, how is your hearing?"

When we arrived home, I made an appointment with Hearing Associates, right next door to Vision Associates. I began wearing glasses in the second grade. I still remember the first time I saw the outline of a leaf. I had on my brand new lenses.

Now I sat in the waiting room of Hearing Associates. The receptionist called my name and, as I entered the examining room, a young woman extended her hand. "Good morning, Mrs. Gilbert. My name is Betsy Cohen. How may I help you?" Even before taking my seat, I began my explanations. "Well, my family doesn't think I'm hearing too well. I had a mastoid operation when I was a year old and I know I miss some things when someone is speaking behind me." I felt like I was rambling. I endured several years before truthfully admitting, even to myself, exactly what I could and could not hear.

I was fitted with hearing aids and, against my better judgment, I got two. Betsy explained that both ears would work more efficiently together. I agreed to try but I was sure that once my mastoid ear had a correction, my hearing would be fine. Anyway, how could I ever adjust to both of my ears feeling plugged?

At my next meeting I sat in the back of the room. Hallelujah. I could hear the secretary read the minutes. As I got up to leave, a friend leaned over and hugged me good-bye. As she put her cheek against mine, there was a loud squeal.

I jerked my head back and mumbled, "I just got hearing aids, and I'm not used to them yet."

As I climbed into my car, I felt unsettled. How can I ever get used to the squealing? Maybe if I leave one out, I can just hug people on the left side. I tried to adjust to the hearing aids, but even voices sounded too loud in closed places, and my ear canals began to itch. I called Betsy and she made some adjustments, but I began to wear them less and less.

I was determined not to feel timid about asking people to repeat comments and questions. I became quite accomplished at asking, always with a note of self-deprecating humor. I returned to the front of the room for meetings and got used to people tapping me on the shoulder when they wanted my attention. Then a classmate from kindergarten called about having a reunion. Could I get to South Carolina for a weekend?

Six of us met at the shore. What a special time for women who had been little girls together! Though our ears were all the same age, more and more I had to request that a sentence be repeated. No one else seemed to have this problem. In bed that first night, I wondered how much of the conversation I had missed. These were exchanges that could never be repeated.

We agreed that our weekend had flown by too quickly. As we hugged good-bye, we talked of our high-school reunion in a couple of months. We discussed losing thirty pounds, what we were going to wear, and other things that grandmothers with little-girl hearts talk about. As my friend and I drove away, I made up my mind to start over at Hearing Associates. I doubted that I could even lose five pounds, much less thirty, but there was no doubt that I did not want to miss one single word at the next reunion—I had to hear it all.

Betsy greeted me with a smile and we made small talk about the last few years. Then I blurted out, "Betsy, I think my hearing has gone downhill and I hate these hearing aids." I began to cry, feeling sad and ashamed. "I just can't wear them. They squeal when someone hugs me, and they make my ears itch." Betsy put her hand on my shoulder. "Let's get you in the box and see what's happening. Then I will tell you how far technology has progressed since you began. I know I can help you."

I leaned toward Betsy as she began to tell me the results of the hearing test. "There is a little progression in your left ear but nothing to worry about. Now, I would like to fit you with a Sequel Tympanette, a deep canal hearing aid. It will be custom made with the precise electronic circuitry to match your individual hearing needs. I will need to make an impression of both your ears. Mrs. Gilbert, you may have as long as you need to see if these are for you."

I left the office with a million conflicting emotions and apprehensions. I would tell no one about this venture. That would be the true test, but very difficult for me. Why did getting older make me feel so vulnerable? But this wasn't about aging. This was about finding a solution to a hearing problem that had begun a long time ago. This new technology was very expensive; however, if successful, I would reclaim a world with sound.

Hearing Associates called within the week. Betsy could see me on Thursday. "The red one goes in the right ear, and the blue one goes in the left ear. Want to give it a try?" I practiced for the next thirty minutes. I walked outside with them. I needed to be certain I could really hear. Then it was time to wear them home. I hugged Betsy good-bye. The right one didn't squeal. I hugged her on the left side. No squeal. When I got in the car, the radio actually sounded too loud. Had I really turned it up that high?

That night as I got ready for bed, I placed this newest miracle in its own case. It was so quiet. I lay in bed thinking about what Betsy had said. I could take as much time as I needed to make the decision. I fell asleep knowing I really only needed two weeks and one major event in my life. By then I would have attended my fiftieth high school reunion.

Everyone I could reach got a hug with no squeals. I heard memories from the man who gave me my first kiss. I heard every note as we sang an old glee club favorite. No one tapped my shoulder. The next morning as I placed the red one in my right ear and the blue one in my left, I felt as though I had been given a gift. The world once more made sense—the sense of hearing.

Lois got much of her world back when she reacquired her hearing. While we seem to depend on sight for so much of what we know of reality, hearing is nearly as vital in providing information for our lives.

In "Terror in the Barn," hearing proves to be crucial to more than just improving the quality of life. At a pivotal moment in the tale, hearing is the key to the survival of man and beast alike.

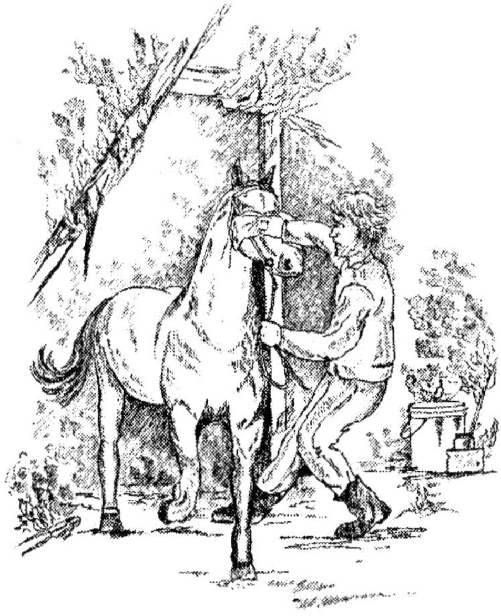

TERROR IN THE BARN

by

Ann M. Cook

When Mike could no longer ignore the wailing siren he flicked off the news cast and glanced at Sharon. She too listened intently as the firetruck approached, the garish lights dancing across the wall of the family-room. When the driver blasted the horn three times Mike leaped to his feet.

"Oh, no! A barn's on fire," Sharon whispered. Mike's thoughts immediately went to their two thoroughbreds, Sweet Baby Jane, heavy with foal, and the big gelding Turbo, their hope for the upcoming racing season. Both horses were stabled at a training facility two miles away.

"Let's go," Mike yelled as they rushed from the house and climbed in the Blazer. With tires screeching they raced after the firetruck.

"The barn...will it burn all the way down? Are there automatic sprinklers?" Sharon asked hurriedly.

"The stable's old. I don't think it's all protected. The new addition is, but not the old part. Being this far from town there's no fire hydrant near."

"I hope someone got the horses out. God...I hope they got them all out."

Long before they arrived they saw the plume of smoke and the flashing lights of several firetrucks. As Mike braked to a stop they saw flames leaping from the windows at the far end of the twenty-stall barn. Smoke seeped from the near entrance as stable-boys and owners led panic-stricken horses from the smoke-filled barn.

"There's Baby Jane. I think she's okay," Sharon yelled. The sorrel mare was circling the holding pen, trying to get to the center of the milling horses, seeking safety within the herd.

Mike and Sharon hurried to the paddock, but were stopped

by one of the firemen.

"Stay back. Get back...you can't go in there," he barked.

Mike scanned the milling horses, but did not see the big bay gelding.

"The bay gelding...the one near the tackroom, is he still in there? He's my horse...I've got to get him out," he shouted.

"You can't go in there, you'll get killed. They got twelve of the horses out. There's only two horses still in there. They can't get to the stall near the tackroom. That's where the fire started," the man said.

Mike looked at Sharon. Her face was ashen, her eyes fear stricken.

"Mike, that's Turbo's stall. Oh, God!" she screamed

"I'm going for him. I have to get him out," Mike yelled. He raced toward the stable, pushing past the fireman who tried to block the way.

Like headlights reflecting off heavy fog, the light from massive floodlights bounced off smoke that billowed from the huge entrance. Elbowing his way to the door, he grabbed a wet towel from a groom, clamped it over his nose and darted through the doorway.

Forty feet into the building, he was aware of an eerie sound, much like air being forced through huge bellows. He paused, then peered into a nearby stall. A shadow loomed on the far side. A horse was backed into a corner. The terrified animal was blowing through flared nostrils, stamping his feet in defiance. With flailing hooves he lashed out at the smoke then again backed into the corner.

"At least I'll get him out of that stall. Head him in the direction of the door. Someone's bound to get him out," Mike thought. He edged forward, calm and unhurried.

"Come on boy...it's not safe in here anymore. You can't fight this, let's get you out," he said.

The horse allowed him to approach and Mike stroked the quivering animal while reaching for the halter.

"Thank goodness he has a halter on," Mike thought.

"Hey. Here...this way. I'll help get him out."

A ghostly figure emerged from the haze. The stable-boy's face was veiled against the smoke, only red-rimmed eyes visible.

"How did you get in here?"

"I sneaked through a side door...I had to try getting these horses out. You ever see and hear a horse burn? I saw one. I don't want to see any more. One's enough."

"I've got to get to the stall near the tackroom...that's where my horse is. I've got to get him out."

"Man...you better get out...them firemen are raising hell about saving these horses. They want everybody out...now! The fire's in the ceiling...they say the whole place is ready to go," the boy said. Mike waved him away.

"Here, you'll need this." The groom handed Mike the damp cloth.

"Get this horse out. Hurry!" As they disappeared Mike went deeper into the barn.

"Turbo...Turbo...," he choked out the words as he stumbled ahead. His legs felt weighted and he staggered, half running, half crawling toward the ever-increasing heat of the fire, drawing in a meager supply of oxygen through the cloth clamped over his nose. Thirty feet farther on he stopped and tried to focus on his surroundings.

Nothing seemed familiar and he crouched lower, feeling along the wall, blindly picking his way. Then over the roar of the fire he heard a horse nicker.

"Turbo! Turbo!" he yelled.

Again the nicker. The horse was close, but Mike had lost his sense of direction. He called again, and again the horse nickered, and Mike plunged toward the sound. He felt the latch of a stall door and fumbled it open.

"Turbo...thank God," he said. The horse was standing quietly, head down, its sides heaving, barely able to stand.

Mike went to the gelding; he grasped the halter and started toward the door. He would get his horse out, this animal who depended on him, this animal that, except for him, might be running free somewhere. The horse balked.

Suddenly there was an explosion of sound like a locomotive barreling through a tunnel as the fire vented through the roof, the updraft sucking smoke and fire skyward in a terrifying red whirlwind.

The horse reared, nearly pulling Mike off his feet.

"God help us!" Mike gasped as an erupting volcano's-worth of searing coals and molten ceiling panels fell about his shoulders. He felt the rush of air that was drawn in through the open door and he whipped the mask from his face, using the still damp cloth to blindfold the trembling horse. He staggered from the stall, yanking on the halter until the horse followed. A hundred feet away a beacon of light pierced the smoke and he turned in that direction.

Behind them timbers popped and crackled as the intense flames claimed the oldest part of the barn. The horse lunged forward. Unable to see, Mike locked his arms around its neck and pulled the blinder from the horse's eyes.

"Go. Turbo...go!" he yelled hoarsely.

The horse raced toward the bright light and the sounds of his stable mates, whinnying in response.

Mike fought to stay conscious as he stumbled along beside the horse as it bolted through the fiery shower. He felt a firebrand on his arm, but was unable to react. Torrents of water washed over them as firefighters flooded the roof of the stable, refreshing him for a moment, the glowing embers hissing underfoot.

His knees buckled and he directed his remaining strength to his arms, holding on while the horse dragged him through the inferno, ever closer to the bright light at the end of the corridor.

They burst into the din of machinery and shouting. A loud cheer blasting his ears was the last thing he remembered. He tried to hold onto the horse, but it pranced away. He lost his grip and fell to the ground.

Then, somewhere through the daze of sub-consciousness, he heard the buzz of conversation and he squeezed his eyes tight to keep out the harsh light. He pushed at the heavy mask clamped over his face and when it didn't move he wearily opened his eyes. Sharon was by his side, but her questioning gaze was on the medic who bent over him. She sighed with relief at his reply.

"He'll be okay...both had a little too much smoke...but they'll be okay," he said.

Although fire is a threat to the main characters in the last story, fire has been a friend to humankind when we learned to control it. It warmed our bodies, cooked our food, and kept away the bigger and stronger predators. Our ancestors first learned to associate fire, ironically, with rain—the fiercest thunderstorms produced downpours and lightning that, in turn, started fires. Ironically, benevolent showers sometimes extinguished the raging forest fires. Today, we understand rain's many other benefits. Rain provides fresh water for drinking, waters our crops, and even helps wash the earth of the toxins we often dump everywhere.

Danny Imwold in "Rain," our next story, looks at neither the ancient view of rain nor our modern understanding of it. His tale is of a rain that, if we're not careful, may be exactly what we deserve for our abuse of Mother Nature.

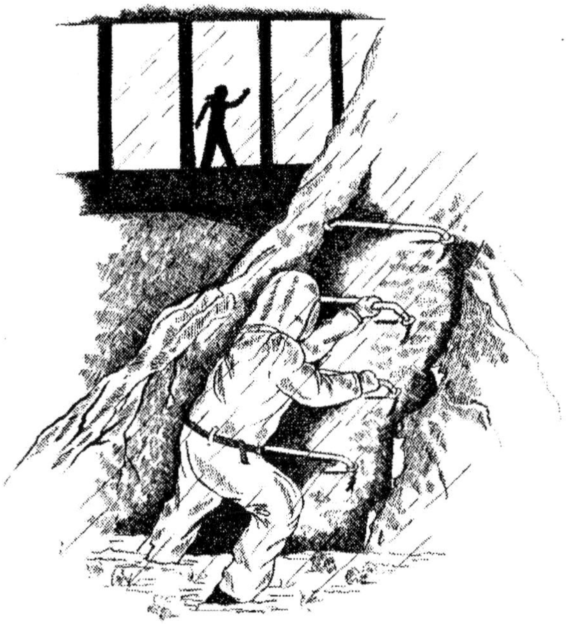

RAIN

by

Danny L. Imwold

He saw the bones just ahead on the parched brown earth, achromatic remains of what had once been a young boy. "Over here," he shouted to his two compatriots. His footsteps marked the hardened soil and whispered away into dust clouds as he approached the ruined leftovers of Billy Haslam, missing since yesterday. He squatted, sweat dripping from his rubber-lined hood, his blue eyes staring through polarized lenses at a face that was no longer there. What remained of young Billy Haslam rested loosely where it had fallen; the ribcage, shoulder blades with the humerus still loose in its socket, lower arm and a few of the carpal bones covered with dust. The skull, including many of the teeth were still there, though the once smooth surface was now pockmarked by what had probably been the last few drops to fall.

"Not much left, is there Doc?"

He looked up into the squinting face of his friend, John Beckett, his long shadow looking like an approaching bus as the dry air blew open his unfastened poncho. His girl-friend and assistant, Paula Newel, the third member of the search party, trudged up behind the big man. "Want me to bag 'em, Doc?" Beckett asked.

Although he'd been born Daniel Oliver Crawford, everyone called him Doc because that's what he was. The only doctor in Shelter 3. He'd come over to 3 at the request of the Governor there when the previous physician had not returned from a hunting excursion two years ago. Paula had come with him and together they had taken over responsibility for the 432 residents of Shelter 3. Together they had delivered twenty-six children, autopsied twenty-nine bodies, salved skin burns on most of the residents, and started a medical school to train his replacement.

"Yeah, John, bag 'im. His parents will want to have the remains before they're cremated. And make sure you get everything, including as many of the teeth as you can find so we can make a positive ID. Run your fingers through the dust for some of the missing ones." There was no reason to dig below the surface; anything there had long dissolved and returned to the soil. Ashes to ashes, dust to dust.

    He stood and walked over to Paula, pulling her poncho up around her neck and pulling the bill of her survival hat down to shield her eyes from the boiling heat of the sun. She reached up and loosened the top of the poncho. "It's too hot, Doc."

    "You know my rule—it stays closed as long as we're out here." He refastened it, then turned to Beckett. "John, close your suit, buddy."

    "Aw, come on Doc, it's like a sauna in this thing. I'll have plenty of time to button up if I have to. And look; there's not a cloud in the sky."

    Doc looked up. The sun had finished its slow plunge beneath the horizon and would soon yield to sparkles of starlight through the night canopy.

    "My rule, John. No exceptions. Things happen too fast out here and besides, you could stand to lose a few pounds in your own personal little sauna." He smiled at his friend.

    "Yeah, yeah," Beckett responded, and stopped gathering the bones long enough to close his survival suit.

    He looked back at Paula, could see beads of sweat trailing down her cheek to her neck, disappearing between her smooth skin and the edge of the poncho. Like everyone who went outside Shelter, she was covered from head to toe in rubber-lined survival gear, taped tightly at the ankles and wrists where rubber-coated shoes and gloves provided more freedom of movement to the appendages they covered. The hat she wore had a pull-down mask beneath the bill with clear polymer covers over the eye slits. A hose connected to an aluminum bottle inside a sealed pocket would provide air for up to half an hour if needed. And like everyone else, she was naked underneath, her body shaved of external hair except for a short coif atop her head. Moisture, sweat, eventually wicked out through specialized materials located in the soles of the shoes, the effect of perspiration cooling the body as God had intended.

    Beckett finished collecting the remains and closed the flap on the rubber and polymer bag to protect the contents. "Ready

Doc," he said. The three turned and headed back to Shelter, its lights glowing now in the muted distance, its polymer dome reflecting the radiance back into its living center.

Doc stood for a moment and reflected on the biospheres of the twelve known Shelters; all self-contained, all located over deep earth aquifers and capable of feeding and housing up to one thousand residents. Three, like most of the Shelters, was significantly below capacity. This was partly due to their original planning, and partly due to the number of autopsies exceeding the number of births. He would have to work on that.

"Come on, Doc," Paula said over her shoulder. He was bringing up the rear, watching her as she walked maybe ten meters in front of him. He could just make out the rounded curves of her bottom, could imagine her breasts sliding up and down inside the sweat-slickened material of the survival suit, her nipples hardening against the rub. He smiled. Yeah, he would have to work on that.

Shelter 3, like the others, looked huge when you got close to it, but was relatively small compared to the open-air cities he remembered as a boy. Then, there were gas-chugging cars, planes, and huge factories producing all manner of goods for consumption. Things changed as he'd entered his teens. Pollution had fogged the major industrial centers of the world, and yellow rain had begun to fall from the skies. The first to suffer were those with respiratory problems, the acridly moistened air burning their already stressed lungs. But as the chemical nature of the rain changed, it began to corrode and burn everything it touched as it fell. Anything metal simply dissolved in a short time. Concrete and steel buildings began to fall. Skin and tissue of anything caught in the open were scalded by the rain. Governments and scientists acted quickly to develop plans for the enclosure of cities in biodomes, similar to those tested in the 1980's. The work, however, had not been quick enough, and hundreds of millions of people around the world had succumbed to the acid rainfall. It was left to the twelve known Shelters, and any others, if there were others, to bring life back to the planet. But first, they would have to wait for centuries of chemical contaminants to be washed from the atmosphere.

"Doc, would you hurry," Paula said again, now nearly shouting to him from thirty meters away. They were approaching the entrance tunnel to Shelter 3, and Doc always felt better when

Paula was inside the tunnel, a male-macho-protective feeling he'd had since the two had moved there. He stopped again and marveled at the engineering that had gone into Shelter.

He knelt to loosen the straps holding his shoes on, trying to cool his feet before entering the tunnel now just fifty meters away. As he released the second strap he felt it. A *thuck* then a splatter on his rain hat. Then another. *Thuck, thuck thuck....*

"Oh shit!" He quickly reached up and pulled his rain mask down over his face, pressing the liner against the seal of the poncho. "Run!" he yelled to Paula, now descending the three-meter high embankment into the tunnel. Beckett had already disappeared into the opening.

"<u>You</u> run!" Paula screamed through her mask.

So he did. The tunnel was surrounded by an embankment designed to stop flooding of the surrounding plateau from entering the biosphere. Acid resistant pumps expelled any waters rising within the enclosure and a chemical-resistant, polymer cover sealed the opening when everyone was safely inside. Daniel Oliver Crawford was not.

The rain fell in torrents, quickly turning the denuded earth into slosh and making it hard for the smooth soles of his shoes to find purchase.

"Dammit, Doc, run!" Paula shouted again.

"Go in," he shouted to her through the downpour, thrusting his arm forward and pointing to the tunnel. "Go! I'll be right there!" He thrust his arm again, and watched as she slid down into the enclosure to the tunnel.

Good, he thought, now I wouldn't have to worry about her.

Reaching the base of the embankment he tried to climb the steps carved into its face but continued to slip and slide in the thickening mud created by the deluge. Reaching for the handholds mounted on the sides of the muddy stair and pushing with both feet, he tried to pull himself up. As he began to make progress, now nearing the middle of the rise, he released his grip on the handhold and lunged for the next higher one.

He missed. Sliding now, bumping against the carved steps, his feet sunk into the mud at the bottom of the embankment and stuck. Sweating profusely inside the suit, he stood for a moment to catch his breath. He activated the reserve air cylinder inside the poncho, then looked up at the challenge before him. Reaching again for the handhold, he tried to lift his right foot to the bottom step. It wouldn't budge. Mud-suck, he thought. He looked again at the handhold and decided that he could pull and jump at the same time, extracting himself from the suction and acquiring the first step at the same time.

"One, two, three..." he whispered. Pulling with his right hand, he jumped.

His naked feet jerked free of the impacted shoes and landed on the step.

At first he felt nothing except the slippery surface of the step. Then he realized what was about to happen.

"Ahhhh!" he screamed into his mask. He lost his grip on the handhold and fell backward into the acid sludge, landing on his rear end and looking up at the embankment. Raising his legs he saw blood and flesh dripping into the muddied earth, the ankle bones and tarsals pushing through the raw meat of his feet. Acid wash began to ooze through the straps he'd loosened at his ankles, mixing with the sweat now puddled at the base of his legs and cauterizing the outer layers of his calf and thigh.

"Oh, God...nooooooo!" he screamed, trying to raise himself from the muck that he was quickly becoming part of. He looked up at the dome, could see Paula pounding frantically at the observation window. He heard the enclosure pumps thrum, disgorging a stream of acidic liquid through the embankment just above him, vomiting its digestive fluid into his mask. He heard the tunnel closure being activated.

Pushing desperately with both hands, he tried to pull himself to the handholds. His feet were gone, the bones of his lower leg now projecting into the corrosive slop surrounding him. The pressure from the pumps had forced some of its effluent through the seals surrounding his mask and he began to feel his skin blistering just beneath the material.

"Oh shit! Oh shit!" He began clawing at the mask, trying to open it, to stop the pain boiling at his chest. Grabbing the taped edge and ripping with his gloved hand, he tore the material free exposing his upper torso to the onslaught of the macerating rain. He tried to scream again, but nothing came out. He looked down and saw flesh melting into the exposed interior of the survival suit, a molten liquor of blood, intestinal fluids, and dissolving tissue.

His body slumped. The rain had seeped down into his arms, melting tendons, muscle and bone. His heart stopped.

*   *   *

John Beckett lifted the weighted survival hat from the base of the embankment and pulled the mask back. The partially digested face of his friend stared up at him.

"Not much left, is there Doc?" he whispered. He began placing the remains into a rubber and polymer bag.

Now, to paraphrase James Taylor, we've seen fire and we've seen rain. Doc's experience with a future downpour proved fatal. Water's more pleasant associations are nowhere to be found in the not-so-great outdoors of this future world.

One of those pleasant associations of water plays as an undercurrent in "Reber's Pond," a wistful tale of a rural family of long ago. For Lila in the story, the social life in the mansion across the lake is just as desirable as Daisy's society was for Gatsby in Fitzgerald's *The Great Gatsby*. Water in both tales is symbolic of the possibility of a rebirth into a new, sublimely happy life. For Gatsby, the dream was tantalizingly close but never attained. Does Lila do any better? Wait and see.

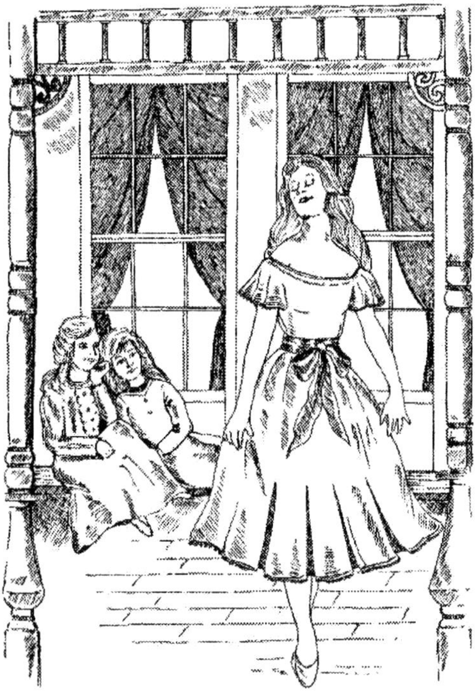

REBER'S POND

by

Ann Cook

The carpenters and stonemasons arrived in early March and from then until the middle of June the sound of hammer and trowel echoed across Reber's Pond.

With them came mammoth, ironclad freight wagons loaded with stone from the quarry just over the hill at Oxford. Day after day the huge drays rumbled past our house causing the walls to shake and the windows to rattle. Burly teamsters cursed as they cracked long black whips over the backs of the sweat-stained, four horse teams.

As I stood on the porch and watched, the thunderous sounds gave me a scary feeling, like being alone on a stormy night.

The wagons labored past our house and around the bend of Reber's Pond to a huge, gray dilapidated building. The once grand manor house now served as a home for old Mr. Reber and as a camp from which he sold fishing supplies and rented out leaky rowboats. Except for our house and one neighbor, Mr. Clark, the camp was the only other sign of habitation in the sweep of brown hills and gnarled woodland that made up the bleak landscape.

The house where we lived—Daddy, Mama, my older sister Tillie and me—was a three-story farmhouse that had its back tucked into a steep hillside. Wooden steps led from a narrow side yard to the second story where a wide porch spanned the full length of the house. The porch overlooked a fenced-in yard, the wire fence covered with honeysuckle and wild-rose, and just beyond the fence, a graveled road and narrow grassy slope formed the border of Reber's Pond.

During the harsh days of early spring some of the workmen drove pilings into the murky, ice-crusted water. Other workers tore away the insides of the camp, creating huge bonfires from the debris, bonfires that flickered at our windows late into the night.

When the weather warmed, Mama, Tillie, and me often walked the short distance around the curve of the pond to watch the progress and to talk to Mr. Reber. It was Mr. Reber himself who told Mama about his plans for the roadhouse.

"There will be a beautiful pavilion extending over the water," he said. His faded eyes sparkled momentarily as he spread wide his arms, embracing his dream.

"Even with Prohibition there will be good food and drink. A romantic place with soft lights, music by famous bands, and dancing. And for those who wish to partake in games of chance...special rooms." He paused when Mama sighed, then winked at her and continued. "You were once a great dancer, you must come and dance for me," he said. His eyes glistened as he word-painted his dream.

On our way home Mama talked of nothing but the new pavilion. "How beautiful it will be, how wonderful to again have a place to dance," she said.

"Teach me to dance. Teach me to dance just like you. Please, please Mama," Tillie said. She stood on tiptoe and glided along the dusty road, arms raised like Mama had done.

"Don't you want to learn to dance like Mama?" Tillie asked me, still teetering on tiptoe.

"I don't think I can learn to dance," I said. It was the only thing I could think of saying. I didn't really want to learn to dance; I wasn't interested. I thought it silly to stand on your toes till they hurt, and I hoped Mama wouldn't insist that I learn. Tillie could be the dancer.

By mid-July all signs of the old camp disappeared, and in its place stood a magnificent stone building with many shuttered windows. A dazzling white pavilion jutted over the water and was even more splendid than Mr. Reber had promised.

As daylight hours lengthened we spent the warm evenings on the porch. The workmen had finished, and now we watched as load after load of supplies was hauled in for the grand opening.

"It looks near ready to open," Tillie said.

"Mr. Reber told me it will open this weekend," Mama answered.

On Saturday, after supper dishes were put away, we hurried to the porch. Tillie and I hung on the rail, gazing at the shiny new touring cars that sped by in a flurry of pebbles. The men were very handsome in dark suits, stiff white shirts and fancy bow ties. Next to them sat doll-faced girls, their flowery gowns exposing snowy bosoms and round, white arms.

Mama watched them pass and, as I sat near her rocking chair, she told us of the time she lived in Philadelphia and danced with the ballet.

She rocked back and forth recounting every moment. Then she paused and took us both by the hand.

"Smeday I will take you to the ballet. We will ride the train and live in the city. We will shop for elegant clothes, eat in fancy cafes, and go the theater every night.

"It will be wonderful to see the city...you can't imagine the city streets at night; they are bright as the stars. A million times brighter than Mr. Reber's pavilion." Her gaze went across the pond to the brightly-lit pavilion.

"When, Mama? When?" Tillie demanded, but Mama waved her aside, sighed and said no more.

When it grew late she tucked Tillie and me into bed and tiptoed from the room. I heard the screendoor squeak as she went back to the porch and then the rhythmic sound of the chair as she waited for Daddy to come home.

For a long time that night, Tillie and I talked of the upcoming trip to Philadelphia. We wondered about the train ride, how many clothes we would have to pack, and where to catch a train.

"I hope Mama doesn't go without us," Tillie said.

"Why would she go without us? She said we would go together. Why would she go without us?" I asked.

"Maybe Daddy won't let us go. I bet Daddy won't let us none of us go," Tillie said. She looked near ready to cry. I reached across to her bed and she took my hand, holding it tight.

"Annie, I won't ever go anywhere without you. Promise you won't go without me," Tillie said.

"I promise. I won't ever go without you. Cross my heart."

I stayed awake for a long time. I wanted to go the city and yet I didn't want to go. Something inside told me if we went to the city we would never come back to this house.

I hoped Daddy wouldn't let us go. I could never be happy living in the city. I wanted to stay here, in this house, in these fields and woods.

And there was Barney, my best friend, the big black Percheron. I loved it when old Mr. Clark hitched his team to the wagon, hoisted me to Barney's broad back and away we went to the fields. I rode for hours, the sun tanning my face and arms, the smell of horses and new-plowed earth deep in my nostrils. How could I be happy about leaving this wonderful place?

Even though I try, I can't remember Daddy being at home very often. Most of my memories are of Mama, Tillie and me.

There were a few times Daddy would come home early. He'd come bounding up the steps, sweep Tillie and me up in his arms and rub his whiskers against our cheeks. He held us both, one on each hip, while asking us questions—many more than we could ever answer. Then he would lower us to the floor and shoo us off to bed.

Then there were nights I would awaken in the dark and hear their voices in the next room.

"But Will...you're never home. We scarcely see you."

"Damn it Lila, you and the girls never want for anything. I give and give and still you're not satisfied."

"I want you to spend more time with us. I'm tired of this lonely life...this boring country life."

"For God's sake, Lila. What is it you really want?"

"Maybe if you came home early we could go to Reber's one night...we could dance...have some fun," Mama said.

"Dancing...is that all you ever think of? You're a married woman with children. You shouldn't even want to go dancing, it's sinful." Daddy's voice was harsh.

"No, I don't always think of dancing. It won't hurt to go, just once. And it's no more sinful than that betting parlor where you hang out."

"That betting parlor gives us a pretty good living, I wouldn't complain if I were you."

"I'm not complaining, I just think you could spend more time at home. We should do things together, do things as a family."

"I know what you want. You want to be back with those bums you call ballet dancers. You'd rather be with them than here with your children. Admit it...that's what you want, isn't it?" Daddy accused.

There was silence, then, "Please, just once take me dancing."

"Please, Will. Please, Will. Is that all you can say? You'd have nothing without me, and you know it. Most women would be happy in your place. You were headed for trouble when I married you. I gave you a decent life. You have a home and two kids, what more can you want?"

"I want to be happy. I want to raise my girls in the city. You brought us to this terrible place and I don't want to live here any longer."

"You'll live here as long as I say, and that's final."

"I hate it here...I hate it. Don't you want me to be happy? Don't you care?"

There was a long silence before Daddy spoke.

"You were doing fine until that old man started feeding you a lot of crap about what a great dancer you were. He doesn't know how I had to put up with all your men friends...those cozy get-togethers with all your men friends. Those 'friends' you put before your husband and children. You're married, and you're going to stay married, you may as well realize that."

After more angry words I would hear the door slam and Daddy's heavy footsteps descending the stairs, and then the sound of the engine as he drove away.

The next day Mama looked tired and her eyes were red and swollen. On those days we never talked about Daddy.

It was on a Saturday. I remember because Tillie and I had just stepped out of the tub and were drying ourselves when Mama came into the bedroom.

"Your daddy will be home early tonight and we'll be going dancing. Tillie, you'll be in charge while we're gone. You're old enough, besides, we'll be over at Reber's if you need us."

When supper was over Mama sent us to the porch while she dressed. I was hanging on the rail when I heard Tillie suck in a long breath. I turned to the door as Mama stepped through.

"Oh Mama…it's beautiful," Tillie whispered.

Mama's dress was the color of a meadow filled with spring flowers. It draped softly to her tiny waist and then billowed into a cascade of delicate petals. Holding the skirt wide she rose to her toes and, like a butterfly hovering on a warm summer breeze, she circled us, the dress a flowing myriad of color. Her bare shoulders were satiny smooth, and her unbound hair, falling midway to her waist, gleamed red-gold in the sun's last rays. Her eyes sparkled like sapphires as she beckoned us with outstretched arms.

Hypnotized by her beauty, Tillie and I rose, and joining hands whirled with her along the length of the porch, back and forth, back and forth, until we collapsed.

I sank into a chair and watched as Mama continued to dance. Raising her arms she began twirling, slowly at first, then faster, her dress and hair swirling, swirling, then falling as she slowed. And again twirling faster and faster, like spring blossoms in a whirlwind, slowing until at last the gossamer threads wafted about her knees.

I stared at her and for a moment wished I could dance. She was so beautiful, all creamy and pink, like a fairy princess, and I held tight to her hand, afraid she might disappear. We begged to stay, but she waved us off to bed.

"I'll just sit here and wait," she said, placing her hands among the folds of the gown.

At first I thought I was dreaming, but the whimper persisted even after I opened my eyes to the darkness. From her deep breathing I knew Tillie was asleep, so I slipped out of bed and down the stairs. I stopped just inside the screen door.

Mama stood at the railing, her slight body racked with sobs.

"Will. You promised. You promised to come home." Her sobs mingled with the music from across the water.

For a time she remained still, then made her way down the steps and through the dew-wet grass. She stopped and looked back briefly before moving through the gate and running along the graveled road toward the pavilion. I went to the railing. I wanted to call her back, but the words wouldn't come. She might take us away tonight and I didn't want to go...I wasn't ready to go. Besides, the music and laughter would drown my cries.

Late into the night I huddled on the porch, watching Mama with her golden hair and flowing dress, dance across the pavilion. Then the damp night air forced me inside and I crept back to bed.

I don't remember going to sleep, but was startled awake by Daddy's loud voice.

"Lila!" he yelled, then again and much louder. "Lila, where the hell are you?"

I lay shivering as I heard him going through the house searching for her. He slammed doors, threw chairs around the room, and finally came bounding up the stairs, the oil lamp wavering crazily. He burst into the room where Tillie and I crouched on our beds.

"Where's your mother?" he demanded.

"I don't know...I don't know, Daddy," Tillie stammered.

I remember that I started to cry and he glared at me.

"Stop it Annie. Stop that crying—right now!" He raised his hand and I shrank away, clutching at Tillie as I scrambled to her side.

"I know where she is," he continued. "She sneaked away to that dancehall. Don't you two move. Stay in the house," he ordered.

He stomped from the room and down the steps.

Over our sobs I heard the door slam and then the roar of the old black Ford as Daddy raced toward Reber's. For the rest of the night Tillie and I shared one bed. We comforted each other and, still holding hands, fell asleep.

"Annie. Wake up. It's time to get up. We promised Mama we'd pick berries today. Come on, get up," Tillie said, shaking my arm. Half awake, I staggered to the kitchen.

We ate a meager breakfast in the silent house before taking our pails to the fields. Daddy had not come home and as we passed the pavilion I sneaked a look. It was deserted.

Several times during the day an uneasy feeling came over me. I knew Mama would not be coming back. Now that she was gone Tillie and I might never see her again.

"Mama's never coming back. She isn't coming back," I said.

"You don't know that. She might be at home right now. She might be wondering where we are, just like we're wondering where she is," Tillie said. She sat beside me and plucked a blade of grass. She chewed the stem, shredding it, then wiped away her tears before continuing.

"She went to the city. She's getting us a place to stay and then she's coming to get us. She'll come for us, wait and see. She'll be here soon, just wait and see."

"I don't think so. She won't come back." I said.

"She told us yesterday she'd take us to the city. Mama wouldn't tell us that if it wasn't so. We have to be ready when she comes. We have to have everything ready to go. She'll be back soon," Tillie said.

"Why did she go without us?" I asked.

"I don't know why, but we have each other. I'll look after you. We'll take care of each other," she said bravely.

I looked at Tillie. She was staring at the blade of grass, tears again staining her cheeks. Then she threw away the grass and helped me to my feet. I wondered if she really believed Mama would come for us.

We filled our pails and it was near suppertime when we passed the empty pavilion on our way home.

As we rounded the bend of Reber's Pond we saw Daddy's dull black sedan parked at the side of the house. He stood talking to the person just inside the screen door. Tillie grabbed my hand and pulled me, stumbling, along the graveled road. We raced up the steps where Daddy waited for us. He caught us up, one in each arm, hugging and kissing us before we wiggled free.

Tillie was the first to reach the door. She stopped abruptly when it opened.

Beneath a mound of snow-white hair, the woman's face wrinkled with a smile. She held out both hands, but Tillie's hand was searching for mine.

Daddy's voice sounded like far-off thunder.

"Tillie, Annie…this is Mrs. Norman. She's here to take care of you till I bring your Mama back."

Tillie turned, searching for me and pulling me to her side. I felt her tremble and I looked into her eyes.

But we had talked about this. Out there in the sunny field, the field filled with weeds and blackberry bushes. We promised to look out for one another. I had to help Tillie. I squeezed her hand and saw the corner of her mouth twitch, like she was trying to smile.

I knew being here without Mama would be bad, but I had Tillie. She needed me. Her dream of going to the city with Mama had shattered, but together, we would help one another. Perhaps Tillie would dance somewhere, someday. For me, there would be no dancing.

Annie may not dance but perhaps she'll grow strong and independent with the responsibility she must assume supporting her sister's dreams. Odd that an activity so positive for so many of us should be negative for Annie.

Our next story, only a moment captured in the life of a character named Sara, features a dance of a most joyous and unusual kind.

DANCING WITH SARA

by

Lois Gilbert

The old man leaned towards the young girl and whispered in her ear. A dazzling smile lit up her face. From the other end of the room a male voice was crooning, "Fly Me to the Moon" as his fingers flew across a keyboard. The old man moved the girl out onto the dance floor. They began to twirl, around and around, backwards and forwards. She threw her head back and one could almost see the laughter that erupted from her throat.
Two other couples moved out onto the dance floor. Louise and I watched silently. The music stopped. The old man took the girl back to a youthful woman who was waiting at a nearby table. The girl who had danced clapped her hands. The woman leaned forward and patted the girl's arm. Louise leaned towards me and spoke quietly, "Her name is Sara and he is her grandfather. The woman is her mother…Sara is retarded and has been confined to that wheelchair all of her life."
The music began again. The man moved behind the wheelchair and once more pushed it out onto the dance floor. Around and around, up and down he pushed the chair. Sara began to laugh and clap her hands. She was seventeen years old and having a dance with her grandfather.

Sara's grandfather seems to derive as much happiness from the wheelchair waltz as Sara does. His enthusiasm reveals both his spirit and his love for his granddaughter. Clearly, he wants to see Sara enjoy life.

"Arcanum," our next selection, also features a man who wants to help a child. This time the child is not related to him—at least not by any bond common to _this_ world. Nevertheless, our narrator struggles to rescue a young boy caught somewhere between heaven and earth.

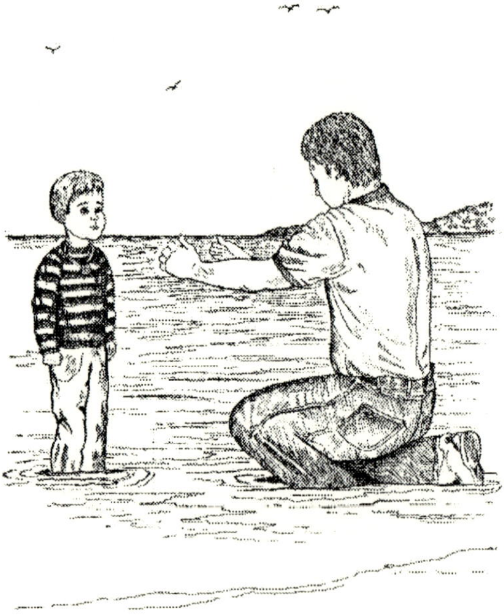

ARCANUM

by

James A. Vella

It was a tiring, mostly unsuccessful day selling religious articles. No, I'm not fanatically religious, but I do wear a medal around my neck. It's gold, two inches in diameter and quite worn; however, with effort, it's possible to make out a heavenly figure spearing a serpent at his feet. The inscription on the back reads: HE SHALL GIVE HIS ANGELS CHARGE OVER THEE TO KEEP THEE IN ALL THY WAYS.

It's always around my neck because it is a valued heirloom and gives me a sense of reassurance.

My mother told me some fantastic stories concerning this medal which, because I dismissed them as fairy tales at the time, I don't remember now. I wish I did.

I was returning home on my usual route along the Coast Road. The air conditioning had quit working before I had gone three miles and the inside of the car became an oven. I lowered the windows, but this helped little in what my dash readout told me was an outside temperature of one hundred twelve.

The heat, the drone of the tires on the hot pavement and the metered bumps in the road combined to mesmerize me. I felt drowsy and began to yawn. I shook my head alert and put my hand outside the window to direct air onto my face which helped only until the sweat evaporated.

No other car was on the road. Strange for a road that is usually busy with traffic. It felt creepy.

My car entered the section of road which is carved into the side of the mountain. On my right, the façade of stone towered to the sky. On my left, far below, silent waves crashed against the boulders on shore and exploded into silvery clouds.

The rhythmic waves of the ocean looked enticing and with concentrated effort, I fantasized wading in them and being bowled over and expected to taste salt on my wet lips.

I considered taking the old Kings Highway down to the ocean and resting a while, but decided it was better to go home, take a cool shower, have an icy beer and watch TV in my air-conditioned apartment. Suddenly, I became aware I had been talking to myself—out loud—and instinctively looked around, embarrassed. I shook my head in disbelief—I had never done that before.

The voice from the car radio was smooth and impersonal. "Police and several hundred volunteers continued their search for seven-year-old Brad Stevensen in the Fowler Woods area. The boy has been missing since yesterday afternoon. Police today reported no trace of the boy but say they will continue the search until dark.

"Kidnapping has not been ruled out, according to police; however, no demand for ransom has been received.

"Mrs. Stevensen today made a personal plea and offered a reward for the safe return of her son.

"Brad Stevensen, when last seen was wearing a red-and-white sweatshirt, blue jeans and tandesert boots. He is three and a half feet tall, has blue eyes and curly red hair. If you have seen this boy please call your local police station"

The story moved me. I pictured the boy wandering about, all alone, lost in the woods—possibly hurt and crying for help.

When I reached down to turn off the radio, I almost lost control of the car—the radio wasn't on!

The hairs on the back of my neck bristled; I could feel sweat trickle along my neck and down my back. I couldn't pull over; a granite rockface crowded the right, and to the left, a rusted steel-wire guardrail barely screened the drop to the waves crashing below. I drove nervously to the Beach Road turnoff. With a tense grip on the steering wheel, I managed to negotiate the winding road parking along the boulders that led down to the tiny beach. I jumped out of the car, and then slipped, slid and mostly fell down the boulders in my rush to reach the ocean.

The water I splashed on my face felt cool and helped calm me. I looked around. The sky was clear, the sun was beginning to set and above the boulders, there was my car. Everything appeared normal, which told me my eyes were all right—but my ears? Hearing a radio that wasn't on?

When I felt calmed, I arose, dusted my clothes and suddenly was startled to see a little boy standing in the shallows. I looked up and down the small beach, but saw no one.

"Little boy, where are your parents?" I shouted.

He looked straight at me but didn't answer. Again I called, "Are you here alone?" When he didn't answer, I approached the water's edge and was shocked to see the boy was dressed in the red-and-white sweatshirt and the blue jeans the radio announcement mentioned.

Now, only a few yards from him, I tried to speak calmly, "You're Brad Stevensen, aren't you?"

There was no response, not even the blink of an eye. He was real all right, but he appeared inanimate, like a manikin.

I waded toward him saying, "You can't stay here, it's going to be dark in a little while, and look at you, you're all wet. Come, I'll take you home."

As I approached him, he slid slowly, smoothly and silently into the water, feet first and hardly creating a ripple. When I lunged to make a grab for him, he had disappeared, but something in the water gripped my wrist and my panic turned to terror.

With all my might, I resisted the pull, but I was slowly being dragged down into the water. My medal glittered as it swung freely from my neck. As I went down, it splashed simultaneously with my scream for help. The hold on my wrist was released so suddenly, I fell backward and wound up sitting in waist-high water. I leaned back, raised my stomach out of the water and crawled backward on my hands and feet, with the jerky movements of a frightened crab…my eyes didn't dare move from that spot in the water…and my chest heaved as I gulped for air.

When safely on the beach, I couldn't stop shaking. I braved walking to the water's edge again and strained my eyes for a glimpse of the boy. Nothing. I was confounded that the boy could submerge, as he did, in less than three feet of water!

Thinking he might have floated from where he went down, I ran along the beach calling his name. There was no sign of him. I doubled back, searching and calling. Again, nothing. I doubled back again, but in vain. I had escaped and the boy had not. I kicked sand in frustration as I crossed the beach.

I slowly climbed the boulders to my car and glanced backward repeatedly in case the boy surfaced and, perhaps somewhat ridiculously, for fear some hideous creature might be following me.

Cautiously, I opened the passenger doors of my car and inspected for any surprises. Satisfied it was safe, I jumped in the driver's seat and started the car. The heat was oppressive and, with the windows closed and my clothes all wet, it felt like a rain forest. I drove well below the speed limit still shaken with what had happened.

Upon entering my apartment, I moved straight to the cabinet and poured myself a two-finger scotch. I immediately felt better—not safe, not calm, not secure—but better.

I traded my wet clothes for my bathrobe with the intention of taking a shower, but instead, poured another scotch and lay on the couch. After finishing my drink, I again put off taking a shower, trying to think, trying to find answers to the questions that ricocheted around in my head. But the harrowing experience and the scotch were too much for me; I fell asleep.

It was dark when I awoke and the questions I went to sleep with were still without answers. I felt confused and groped for some action to take; call the police? No, they would never believe the story. I picked up the phone and called my doctor-friend, Henry Pieler. The slow drawl of his words told me he had been asleep.

"I need to talk to you."

He yawned and said, "Talk."

"Not on the phone. Can I come over?"

"After...midnight?"

"Yeah...please, it's important!"

After a long silence, he said, without enthusiasm, "If you say it can't wait, it can't wait...so, come on down."

Henry opened the door. His open bathrobe drooped like an old blanket over his wrinkled pajamas. His thin hair was disheveled and his eyes were only half opened. He stifled a yawn with the back of his hand and said, "Are you sure this can't wait 'til morning?"

I shook my head emphatically.

He led me into his study and I anxiously recounted my experience; he appeared to be struggling to stay awake.

"Henry! You weren't listening to me."

He opened his eyes wide, asserting, "Yes...yes, I've heard every word. So, what do you want *me* to do?"

"Well, what do you think happened?"

"I think you had a daytime dream, accompanied by hallucinations. It's happened to people before, many times. In your case, I suspect it was the heat. I suggest you go home and get some sleep. In the morning, if you don't agree with what I just said, call me and we'll talk some more."

"But Henry, I know I experienced it!

"Tom, I can't help you with this when I'm half asleep. Right now, I can only advise you to go home and get some sleep yourself."

My disappointment and desperation must have been apparent. "...Can't sleep anymore, I need something more than 'call me in the morning'!"

Henry's slippers flapped against his bare feet as he scuffed to his desk. He picked up a prescription pad and scribbled with his desk pen. "Here, stop at a drug store and get this filled. Take two and go to bed. In the morning, if you want, call me."

I awoke on the couch. My head ached, my leg felt like it was being pricked by a million needles and the inside of my mouth felt like it was full of the cotton that came in the pill bottle.

The sun's rays beamed through the window and bounced around the room in comforting brilliance. The alarm clock read 10:30. Daylight made a difference. It dispelled the spookiness of the previous day, but it didn't change my conviction that what I experienced the previous day was real—it was not a dream or a hallucination—and no one was going to tell me differently!

When I called, Henry didn't seem surprised, he simply said, "My office, 1:30, okay?"

When I entered, Henry smiled indulgently, extended his right hand to shake mine and motioned to a chair with his left. He looked different today, especially his hair. He was prematurely balding. A wreath of hair circled his head from ear to ear and a few strands had been allowed to grow long enough to comb across the top of his head. The deeply embedded metal bridge of his glasses gave the appearance it was the cause of his hooked nose. As he walked to his chair, he asked, "How are you feeling, okay?"

"Yeah, I'm fine," I said.

He sat with his elbows on the desk and his hands clasped under his chin. He smiled that somewhat patronizing smile and said, "Now tell it to me again."

While I was recounting my experience, he didn't seem to be paying attention. He played with a pencil, then rearranged things on his desk and finally swiveled his chair around to look out the window—with his back to me.

When I finished, he stood up, furrowed his brow as he walked around and sat on the corner of his desk. He pursed his lips, nodded several times and said, "Like I said last night..." I interrupted, "But what about the voice coming from the radio? It wasn't on! I just told you."

"Ah, but I think it *was*. You heard the news story and while you were concentrating on the image of the boy lost in the woods, you unconsciously turned off the radio. Then, when you *consciously* went to do so, you found it off. Look, did you ever get in your car, drive a few miles and then wonder if you locked you apartment or turned off the lights? I'm sure you have."

"Now, as for the rest of it: you had an unsuccessful day. The air conditioning quit. It was very hot. You were alone on the road and, most importantly, you thought you heard a radio that wasn't on. Therefore, as you lay in the sand, these things sparked your imagination to concoct the hallucination."

I thought about what he said. It was reasonable, "You could be right," I muttered.

"To be fully convinced, I want you to do something; go back to that very spot. Lie in the sand or walk along the beach...even take off your shoes and socks and wade. Spend a little time there and I guarantee you'll come back assured I'm right."

That sounded like good advice: "If you fall off the horse, get right back on."

I parked my car along the side of the road, just like the first time. I climbed down to the beach and, like the day before, it appeared to be deserted. On such a beautiful day, with the temperature at ninety-two, I took off my shirt and lay on the sand with my fingers interlocked behind my head. The stirring breeze, patterns of high, thin clouds and the steady roll of the waves didn't help me relax. I closed my eyes but blinked them open repeatedly expecting...I don't know what.

No use trying to relax. I got up and shielded my eyes against the setting sun. The scene appeared exactly as it did before and, to my shock, the boy was there, standing in the shallows! I rubbed my eyes in disbelief and looked again. He was there all right; he had hardly changed from his first appearance. He was dripping wet and, despite the warmth of the day, he was hunched in a freezing pose. His wet hair was without curl and clung to his head like a helmet. His frightened expression and opened mouth gave me a sense he was—without sound—screaming for help.

The rays of the setting sun reflected from my medal and played small circles of light on the boy's face. I saw him blink once.

"Little boy, are you all right? Can you move? Speak to me!"

He didn't answer.

I walked toward the water and the reflection from my medal now danced on the water at the boy's feet. I saw a slight twitch of his leg. I was encouraged but was at a loss what to do next. The reflected light found and stayed on a medal the boy wore around his neck, and there was a blinding flash, like an electrical short circuit. The boy came rushing toward me as if being pushed and resisting the force. He unexpectedly jumped out of the water, landed at my feet, turned abruptly and raced along the water's edge, running at unbelievable speed.

It happened so fast, I was left dumb. I regained my voice, cupped my hands at my mouth and shouted, "Hey, little boy, wait...I'll take you home!" But by that time, the boy was kicking his legs high and then jumping from one boulder to another on part of a jetty extending into the ocean. He disappeared behind the jetty, away from the water. I shook my head and grimaced in defeat; I had lost him again. But this time I lost him on land.

I stared at the ocean, confounded by its below-surface enigma. I smiled wryly, remembering Henry's words.
Climbing back to my car, I had a vague and inexplicable feeling of victory.
I awoke the next morning feeling good, like my old self. I made breakfast and unrolled my newspaper as I started to eat.
The headlines screamed: BRAD STEVENSEN IS SAFE! Pushing my breakfast aside, I read eagerly. The boy could not recount any detail of the days he was missing...his mother was quoted as saying he walked in the front door as if he hadn't been missing at all. A picture of Brad showed a medal around his neck.
I unconsciously reached for mine, the twin of the one in the picture, and it was gone.
I returned to the beach halfheartedly, not so much to look for the medal as to remind myself there are worse things to lose.

Brad Stevensen is found and rescued by a man who finds not only the boy but his own faith as well. The lost party in "A Gift for Benjamin," however, is not a boy but a boy's dog. Maggie's return becomes nearly as important to Benjamin's family as Brad's return was to his.

In this next tale, the angels are empathetic human beings who know that treasured pets become loving members of the families to whom they bond. The loss of a furry family member can be devastating. The loss can be even more traumatic if one of the family members is responsible.

A GIFT FOR BENJAMIN

by

Ann M. Cook

"Wow! It's cold…cold enough to snow!"

The words were lost in the blustery December wind that brought banks of dark clouds sweeping in from the West. David looked at the threatening sky, momentarily forgetting the buff-colored spaniel that he had just released from the confines of the house. On remembering her, his gaze searched the winter-browned fenced-in yard but she was nowhere in sight. He noticed the gate; it was ajar. He anxiously scanned the adjoining woods.

"Maggie! Here, Maggie. Come here girl," he called into the early morning. He waited. When she did not appear he looked at his watch and hurried into the house.

"Where's Maggie? I heard you calling her," Barbara said.

"Mom, the gate was left open and she got out. She's in the woods and wouldn't come when I called. Who left the gate open?"

"I don't know, and anyway, nobody ever admits leaving it open. Both you and Benjamin are equally guilty of that," Barbara said.

"Guilty of what?" Benjamin asked, coming into the kitchen.

"Guilty of leaving the gate open. Maggie got out and wouldn't come back for David."

"I'll call her. She'll come for me," Ben said, giving David a superior-to-you look.

"Not now, you don't have time. She'll be here to meet the bus when you get home; she's never missed it yet," Barbara said.

She handed the boys their lunch. They quickly stored them in backpacks. She watched as they slammed the door and bounded down the steps, each accusing the other of leaving the gate unlatched.

Benjamin favored his mom. Her raven hair and slight build, her fair coloring and fine facial features. But instead of her brown eyes, his were the deep blue of a summer evening sky and thick lashed beneath wing-shaped eyebrows. Conversely, though two years younger, twelve-year-old David was two inches taller, more robust in build, and with a shock of brown hair that mirrored that of Stan, Barbara's husband. Barbara felt a rush of compassion and wished she could have assured them both that Maggie was sure to be home when they returned.

When Maggie was let out of the house she eagerly scoured the yard from front to back. Finding nothing of interest she was quick to discover the open gate and, before David noticed, she was out and racing toward the woods. There, her keen nose immediately picked up the fresh scent of a rabbit. Her bobbed tail wagged furiously as she followed the fleeing rabbit, first through the woods, then into neighboring fields before it circled back to the woods.

She was closing the distance to the rabbit when she heard David calling and she hesitated. Suddenly she sighted a deer and, forgetting David and the rabbit took up pursuit of the six point buck. The buck skirted the scattered bungalows in the village and fled toward the Government installation a half mile away.

On reaching the Cyclone fence surrounding the Army base, Maggie squeezed through a hole and lost the trail. Seconds later she again sighted the deer and again her hunting instinct was all that mattered. She barked with excitement, her head high, the object of the hunt only yards ahead, apparently within easy reach.

The young buck made a game of the chase, bouncing through frosty fields and woodlands while he led Maggie farther and farther from home. He stayed just ahead, teasing her with false hopes, letting her glimpse the white flash of tail, hear the rattle of leaves and the crackle of underbrush.

Throughout the morning whenever Maggie rested the buck also rested. By early afternoon he tired of the chase and, to elude the persistent dog, he headed for his last bastion - the salt marsh of the Gunpowder River. He sprinted along the edge of a stubble-filled cornfield bordering the marsh, down a five foot embankment and onto a hammock dense with cattails and marsh grasses. He stood motionless and waited to see if the dog followed.

Fifty feet downwind Maggie came to a stop on the high bank and sniffed the air. In front of her the marsh stretched lonely and cold toward the Chesapeake Bay. Where the swaying grasses met the open water a duckblind squatted haphazardly, seemingly ready to collapse. A brisk wind churned the surface of the gray-green water into a froth of whitecaps.

Then Maggie picked up the scent of something alien. No longer was there the scent of deer, or the woodsy smell of decaying leaves and moss. Now the air reeked with the heavy odor of muskrat, and she snuffled at the unfamiliar scent.

Suddenly from her vantage point she saw a flash of brown as the buck sprang from the hammock into shallow ebb-tide water. In a final spurt of pursuit Maggie slid down the embankment into a small tidal pool. As her feet hit the water she felt something other than river mud under her left forepaw, and before she could react the steel jaws of the leg-hold trap snapped shut, gripping her leg just above the dew-claw.

Jerked to a stop she tumbled into the water. Stunned, she got up and shook herself. She started toward the bank, but the chain anchoring the trap was short and again she was yanked into the water. For the first time she felt the sharp pain and as she lifted her foreleg the acrid smell of blood mingled with the smells of the marsh.

She quickly learned that to ease the pain she needed to stay close and not pull against the weight holding her fast, so for a long time she remained still.

As the tide turned she became uneasy. She sensed Benjamin and David would be looking for her and she tried to pull free, only to have the trap cut deeper. She could not escape the steel grip that held her prisoner.

Once during the long hours from across the river came faint sounds of duck hunters. She barked sharply, ears pricked toward the distant voices. She waited, but soon there was no sound other than the rustle of dry grasses and the twitter of redwinged blackbirds as they returned to the safety of the marsh. She fell silent.

Relentlessly the rising water buffeted her, staining her pale coat a muddy brown. It threatened to engulf her, occasionally filling her nose and mouth with brine, and she paddled furiously. The heavy trap moored her to the river bottom. She whimpered each time a wave washed over her and, like a cork weighted with a lead sinker, she bobbed on the flowing tide. As she struggled to keep afloat snow sifted from the leaden sky.

The light coating of snow crunched underfoot as Benjamin quietly closed the door and made his way across the frozen deck. From the topmost step he surveyed the yard then drew a deep breath and directed a sharp whistle toward the wooded area behind the house. He paused, blew warm breath on his cupped hands and shouted into the evening silence.

"Maggie! Here Maggie! Come on girl! Come on Maggie!"

For a long minute he listened intently. He hoped for sounds that would suggest the spaniel had heard. He half expected her to burst from the woods, race across the yard and come bounding up the steps. As he watched hopefully, his slim frame trembled in the snowy dusk and he rubbed his arms in an attempt to help circulate warmer blood to his frigid hands.

He stayed until the twenty degrees made it impossible to remain outdoors with only a flannel shirt for protection. He sighed and returned to the warmth of the big kitchen. Barbara and David watched as he closed the door and sank into a chair.

"Mom, she's not coming home...she's not _going_ to come home. How come she won't come home Mom?" he said. Tears welled and he brushed them away, hoping David would think they were caused by the cold air.

"She's been off hunting before; try not to worry," Barbara said, turning from the stove where she tended an assortment of steaming pots. She tousled Benjamin's dark hair and touched his cold-reddened cheeks.

"Mom's right. She's probably on her way home right now," David said from across the oval table.

"How do you know. Just how do you know. You probably don't care if she _never_ comes back. _You're_ the one who let her loose this morning!" Benjamin glared at his sibling.

"I didn't mean to...Mom...tell him I didn't mean to!"

"Both of you. Stop it. Benjamin, I'm sure David didn't think Maggie was going to run off."

"He shouldn't have let her out of the yard...why didn't he watch her and not let her get out!" Benjamin pleaded. His voice shook, partly from uncontrolled shivering and partly from sobs.

"Mom, I didn't do it on purpose. She's been loose before and never ran off; besides, I didn't notice the gate was open, she was gone before I could stop her," David said. He slammed shut his math book and stomped out of the kitchen. They heard his heavy footsteps on the way to the upstairs bedroom.

"Mom, I know something's happened to Maggie. She never stayed away this long before. It's dark. It's cold; maybe she's hurt. Maybe she's laying in the snow and can't get home. What can we do, Mom?"

"I don't know...when your Dad gets home you can go look for her. I have no idea where she could be." She knew Benjamin was trying not to cry openly.

"Mom...what about her puppies? What will happen if she's going to have puppies?"

"Benjamin, we don't know if she's going to have puppies: it's too soon to tell. She'll be okay, she won't hurt herself."

"She'll come home...won't she, Mom?" Benjamin asked. He picked up the new red collar that was Maggie's Christmas present and on which already hung her identification tags. The red leather collar cost him most of his allowance.

Yes, she'll come home...if she's able, Barbara thought.

Through the feathery snow Clint strolled along the river road. The wind was dying, its bite ceasing, but December's deep freeze had settled in. Today, as was his custom during the week, he jogged the two miles from work to the end of the dirt road at the wetlands. On his return he slowed to a walk in order to enjoy the quiet of the woods and marsh. He relished the stillness of twilight: it rested his mind and soul, took him away from the computer terminal and the pressure of a job that took too much of his time.

Suddenly, he stopped to listen. There was a sound from near the water, a sound he couldn't quite identify. He paused, focused on any sound other than the wind and leaves. Then, as the wind direction changed, he heard the muffled barking and he ran to the river's edge.

"Oh my God," he whispered.

With only rump and head above the lapping water Maggie looked to him, whining in expectation. Clint dropped to his knees and reached for the scruff of the neck as she strained toward his hand. He lost his hold when the steel tether jerked her from his grip.

"Damn, what's the matter? Are you caught on something?"

He grasped the sodden hair again, but when he pulled, Maggie yelped and he released his hold, only to see her sink beneath the murky water. She popped to the surface moments later, choking, eyes bulging with fear.

Maggie tried to pull herself toward Clint as he slid down the bank into the ice-cold knee-deep water. He cradled her weary head and beneath his hand felt her quiver with fright and cold. For a minute she rested against his warmth, staring with white-rimmed eyes, pleading. After a time he freed his right hand and, when he discovered the chain she yipped in pain.

"Okay boy...take it easy...I'll get you out of here." Clint slowly traced the chain to where it was fastened to an iron stake driven into the base of the bank. Only a stub of the stake was exposed. He let his hand retrace the length of chain, hoping to find a clasp that would separate the trap from its anchor. The chain links were solid and uninterrupted. He tested its strength, but the chain held. He tried several time to loosen the stake, but it was driven deep.

The river continued to fill. Maggie's nose now barely above the frothy waves. With one hand Clint held her head, stretching the little neck to its limit. He knew this animal's life depended solely on him and he silently prayed for strength.

Clint took Maggie's leg and felt for the trap. At the pressure on the injured leg Maggie cried and pulled away. To loosen the stake would take both hands and Clint knew it may mean the dog would be under water once he let go its head. The high-water mark on the muddy bank told him the tide was only partially in and he cringed at the thought of watching the dog drown. The trap or the stake, either way there were only minutes left. He winced as he let go her head.

Maggie thrashed, churning the water, her eyes wide. She succeeded at times to get a mouth full of air as she struggled, then went under, her body convulsing as she fought to get to the surface.

Clint groped for the stake and, when its jagged head cut into his palm, he felt the sting of salt water in the wound. As Maggie fought for life her sharp claws tore at his arms and he lost his grip.

He sank to his knees and though knowing it would pull the dog deep into the water, he twisted the chain around his right wrist and tugged. He put his weight against the stake, forcing it this way and that, whipping it side to side, willing it out of the ground.

He became aware the dog stopped fighting and a cry of determination escaped clenched teeth. He no longer noticed the freezing water or numb fingers. He grappled with the chain, groaning with the effort, strained muscles contorting his neck, face twisted in anguish. He fought the stake for what seemed an eternity but was, in fact, only the longest minute of his life. After a violent tug it pulled loose sending him backwards.

Maggie floated to the surface, pale fur wafting like a halo, and over the night sounds of the marsh, an eerie silence.

Quickly Clint swept the small creature up and splashed to shore, heaving his burden onto the bank. Climbing up he began pushing on the little ribs, hoping to pump water from the lungs, not knowing for sure it would help. Occasionally he stopped to see if there was life. He labored over the dog until his arms ached. He paused and freed the injured leg. He hurled the trap far into the marsh before gathering the limp animal in his arms.

Benjamin was in the driveway when the Blazer came to a stop. His Dad was home.

"Dad...Maggie's gone. She's been gone all day. Mom said you'd know where to look for her," he cried, pulling open the door.

Stan saw the terror in Ben's face. "Hold on...Ben, calm down. What's happened?" he asked, sliding from the Blazer. He listened as Benjamin told how the spaniel hadn't come home and how afraid he was that something terrible happened to her.

"Go tell Mom we'll eat dinner later...after we look for Maggie," Stan said, pulling himself back in the driver's seat. Benjamin ran to the house and Stan could hear his excitement as he told Barbara of their plans. Ben raced back to the truck.

Stan drove slowly, the headlights piercing the darkness. Benjamin scanned the snowy roadside on their way to the village. Stan brought the Blazer to a stop at a dark-shingled house on the far end of the village. "Maybe Jack will have seen her," he told Benjamin.

The back yard was ablaze with light and they found the old trapper in the skinning shed. At the door they were greeted by a surge of heat from an old wood stove and a nod from the man bent over a scarred oak table. Stan quickly told of the missing Maggie. When he paused Jack thumped the table with the butt of his knife. He looked at Benjamin with raised eyebrows.

"Damn, I hate to hear that. Is she in heat? Maybe she's with a male somewhere. If she is, I wouldn't worry too much, she'll be back in a day or two."

"You're probably right, but she's Ben's dog and he's worried about her. She's never been gone this long and we thought maybe she was seen in the village."

"Not that I know of. Nobody mentioned seeing a dog around here."

"Mr. Jack, we think Maggie might be going to have puppies, right Dad?" Ben said.

"Yes, she was bred several weeks ago and she might be with young, but it's too soon to be sure," Stan replied then added, "We'll go home and wait. She'll show up soon."

"Ben, would you go ask my wife to send the sharpening tool, I need to sharpen this knife," Jack said.

When Benjamin left, Jack closed the door and faced Stan.

"God, I hate to tell you this, but I did hear talk about a dog—it got caught in a trap at the river. Caught in a leg-hold. I don't know what kind of dog it was. I sure hope it wasn't yours...you know what a leg-hold does."

"A trap. What would Maggie be doing at the river? That's a long way from home. She's never gone that far. And how would she get through the fence?"

"Hell, there's no trouble getting through the fence. There's lots of holes...big ones for deer, little ones for rabbits...been cut in there by poachers. Poachers cut the fence and then wait outside for the deer, that's how they make a kill every year."

"But it couldn't be Maggie. God, not here at Christmas. It would kill Ben if anything happened to that dog," Stan said.

"I don't know, but what I heard was a jogger found a dog that was caught in a trap. I don't even know if it was a female, only that it was found."

"God...I hope it wasn't Maggie."

"I do too."

"Thanks Jack. It's somewhere to start. If it's her, we'll find out. If it is Maggie, maybe she's okay. I won't say anything to Ben right now. I don't want to get his hopes up, and I sure don't want him to think she might be dead."

"Check with the Post vet on Monday, maybe someone turned in a dog. If I hear any more I'll let you know," Jack said carefully as Ben came in and handed him the sharpener.

Benjamin climbed in the Blazer. "Dad, what can we do?"

"Nothing right now, we'll start on Monday...except for searching the entire county, I don't know where to look. In the meantime we'll check the paper the next two days. Jack said the Post vet might know something, or maybe she's at the pound." He glanced at Benjamin who huddled in the corner, teeth chattering from the cold.

"Dad. What if Maggie is lying out in the snow? What if Maggie is lying somewhere dead...in the snow," he stammered.

Stan pulled Benjamin close, holding him and feeling him shudder.

"We have to hope she's okay, it isn't good for you to think those things Ben. We have to keep faith that she's alright."

"Dad, you don't suppose Maggie is waiting at home now; maybe she's waiting for us to show up," Ben said hopefully.

"You never can tell. Maybe she is."

On the drive home Benjamin stared out the window. Once he yelled to his Dad to stop when the headlights shone on a discarded pasteboard box. It proved to be empty. When home and not greeted by Maggie, he wordlessly trudged to the house. After silently picking at his supper, he pleaded fatigue and went upstairs.

The visit to the Post vet on Monday morning provided no record of a spaniel having been brought in, nor did the inspection of the pound's twenty cages reveal Maggie. A strained quietness between Benjamin and David prevailed. Not even the start of Christmas vacation was celebrated by either boy.

"Tonight we trim the tree," Barbara announced during supper.

When the tree was in place, she eagerly assigned each a task, but the event that always brought the brothers closer was sadly quiet. They were driven apart by Maggie's absence.

Back in the kitchen Benjamin stood at the door. He gazed past the holly-wreath, past the Christmas lights, out into the starless night.

"Oh no! Mom...it's snowing again. What if Maggie's out in the snow?" he cried, turning to Barbara with fear stricken eyes. Without waiting for a reply he fled to his room.

Barbara started after him then glanced at David. He slumped in the chair, staring at the tablecloth, eyes filled with tears. David looked at the cloth, his forefinger traced the outline of a poinsettia. Teardrops lay like diamonds on the red plastic.

"Mom...I don't know what to say to Ben. He hates me for what happened; he thinks I let Maggie out on purpose. He doesn't know I miss Maggie just as much as he does."

"No David, no, Benjamin doesn't hate you. Believe me."

"Mom, Christmas is only four days away. I want to give Ben a present...I want to bring Maggie home so Ben will be happy. It could be my gift to him. How can I get her back Mom?" David said. He rested his head on the table and sobbed. "It's Christmas...it's supposed to be a happy time, without Maggie it won't be happy."

Barbara could find no words of comfort.

The quiet of the moment was broken by the ringing of the phone. She picked it up glad for the interruption. It was Jack asking for Stan. She handed the phone to her husband.

"Stan, I got someone here maybe you should talk to. Sorry it's so late but he says he knows about the dog that got caught in the trap. Here, talk to him...." Jack said. His voice slurred and Stan knew he must be at his favorite bar. There was a silence then a voice boomed over the line.

"Stan...Jack says you lost a dog and I might be able to help you. The fellow that found a dog lives near me. His name's Clint. I don't know his last name, but I can give you directions to his house."

Stan jotted the information on a pad of paper and, motioning to Barbara, held the receiver so she too could hear.

"I ain't seen it, but I do know Clint found a female dog. Could be it's the one you're lookin' for. Seems Clint couldn't bring himself to leave the dog at the pound. It was more dead than alive and he didn't want her destroyed if she did live and nobody claimed her...he fell in love with that dog...." The booming voice dissolved in a burst of music. Stan yelled a thanks, hung up and folded the bit of paper. He put it in his pocket.

"Do you think it might be Maggie? I prayed we'd find her," Barbara said, squeezing his arm. "I'll tell the boys."

"No...not yet. Maybe we'd better wait till after the holidays, at least until I talk to Jack directly. I know how people confuse things, especially when they've had too much holiday cheer. The boys will be too disappointed if it isn't Maggie. At least they still have hope of finding her. If this lead fizzles out there won't be anything left."

I know, but suppose it is Maggie; there's always that chance...isn't there?"

"Let's wait. Leg-holds drown the animals. She may have died. I don't know what we can do to get the boys over the feelings they have, maybe after Christmas..." he stopped when David appeared at the doorway.

"Dad, I heard. We've got to find out if it's Maggie. Please Dad, let's go see if it's Maggie. It'll only take a little while, then we'll know for sure. Please Dad."

"Stan, take him. The worry is worse than not knowing...whatever the outcome it's best to know. David knows that too," Barbara said looking directly at David.

"Get your coat. We'll go see, but don't get your hopes up, there's a good chance it won't be Maggie. They hurried out to the truck.

"Dear God...Please let it be Maggie. Let her be alive," Barbara said quietly as she watched the Blazer pull out.

Through a fairyland of shimmering snow and Christmas lights neither of them noticed, David and Stan made their way to an uncertain end.

"Dad, I'm praying that it's Maggie. It has to be her, it has to be Maggie!" David's voice broke with emotion.

"David, don't blame yourself for what happened. If we find it isn't Maggie, we'll keep looking. Hopefully someone's found her and taken her in. They'll probably advertise in the paper. We'll keep looking and hoping for the best."

"But Dad, it has to be Maggie. I made a promise to myself I'd bring Maggie home. It has to be her. I don't want Ben to be sad."

"I know you feel responsible, but Ben is hurt—that's why he's angry. It could easily have been him that let her out. Okay?" Stan looked at his youngest son.

"It'll work out. One way or another...it'll work out." He patted David's knee.

He checked the number on the mailbox before turning onto the snow-covered driveway.

The dog lay on her belly, her soulful gaze trained on the crackling fire. At every sound she cocked her head, ears pricked, and, not recognizing a familiar sound, she relaxed and again stared at the flames.

From a nearby chair the man watched, saw her velvety brown eyes slowly turn in his direction. Her eyes closed and she whimpered. He went to the kitchen and returned with a dish of food.

"Come on girl, you have to eat...it's nearly four days and you haven't had much. You're getting thin, awfully thin."

He placed the dish near the dog's nose but not even the enticing smell of beef stirred her.

Suddenly her ears pricked. She stood. Her eyes brightened and her abbreviated tail wagged, stopped, then wagged furiously. Her ears were attuned to the sound of the vehicle coming up the drive.

"You know who that is, do you girl?" the man put aside the magazine and went to the window. A gray Blazer came to a stop and, as he waited for the knock at the door, he knelt beside the dog. He gently scratched her head smoothing the silky topknot.

"This may be goodbye girl. It's not turning out the way I hoped. I knew you belonged to someone and they'd be looking for you. I can't keep you knowing others are grieving."

The dog's gaze followed as he went to the door. When it opened she was there instantly, jumping, spinning, first at David then Stan, barking excitedly. David dropped to the floor, capturing her, holding her tight, his face against the squirming body.

"Oh Maggie...wait till Ben sees you. He'll be so glad. Wait till Ben sees you. Dad, Ben will be so glad...so glad," he cried.

For a moment both men were silent. Clint was the first to speak.

"I hoped she could stay with me...be mine. I also knew she would never be happy. I'm glad you're here." He told of getting Maggie out of the river and taking her to a nearby vet. "Except for a fairly deep cut that's healing nicely, she's in great shape." He watched an adoring Maggie nuzzle David's neck, wash his face with a wet tongue and snuggle in his arms.

Stan saw the sorrow in Clint's eyes.

"We're planning on Maggie having a litter of puppies. Our family would like to make you a gift of a puppy if you'll accept one. It'll be our way of saying thanks. It's mighty sad in our house without Maggie...right David?"

"I hoped no one would be looking for her, that she might be abandoned for some reason, but I knew that wasn't likely. Yes, I <u>will</u> accept your offer. I'd like a female, the more like Maggie the better. She'll have a good home; I'll guarantee that," Clint said.

"Thank you Mister Clint, thank you for saving Maggie. My brother and me will pick the prettiest puppy for you," David said from where he wrestled with a happy Maggie.

Clint closed the door and through the window watched Maggie run to the Blazer. She turned and raced back to the father and son as though to hurry them along.

Through the windshield David saw the brilliant lights of Christmas and knew Benjamin's eyes would outshine them all. He had his gift for Benjamin.

Benjamin and David find their Maggie, an occasion for celebration. Certainly, a child finding a lost dog is a cause for rejoicing. How much happier an occasion, JoAnn M. Macdonald asks, when a child finds God?

The true story of the first American woman to be ordained by a congregation is a story of a child's discovery of deep faith and a religious calling. Moreover, Antoinette Brown discovered that the struggle to do what God had in mind for her would be the challenge of her lifetime.

A LITTLE CHILD WILL LEAD THEM

by

JoAnn M. Macdonald

Nettie Brown was eight years old when she heard Charles Grandison Finney preach. He was a dramatic speaker, one of the early revivalists. When he spoke he touched the hearts of his listeners. Hers was one of them. He told the congregation of sinners about the Lord and his forgiveness, and how they should give their lives to the Lord. Elizabeth Cazden wrote in her book *Antoinette Brown Blackwell* that Nettie was so excited to think she could give her life to the Lord that she told her Sunday school teacher she wanted to be a minister.

"Nettie," her teacher said rather mockingly, "you *can't* be a minister because you are a *girl*."

Nettie was crushed. She was so sure that she *could* be a minister like Preacher Finney that she could hardly wait to get home to tell her mother what the teacher said.

Her mother saw the fire of inspiration in her young daughter's eyes. She recognized in her daughter the exuberance of youth and the determination to do what she chose to do. A strong woman in her own beliefs, Abby Brown wanted Antoinette to be everything she could be. She wanted her daughter to reach her God-given potential. She would help her in any way she could.

Abby was a gentle lady. She stroked Nettie's hair and hugged her as she said, "Antoinette, you can be anything you want be. If your dream is to be a minister, then wear this ribbon under your collar. And when someone tells you that you can't be what you want to be then you hold fast to this ribbon. You hold on to your dream, as long as it takes." Her mother's eyes were serious when she looked straight at Nettie. She pinned the white ribbon inside Nettie's collar. It was the confidence Nettie needed to stay focused—to be what she wanted to be.

Antoinette was born in 1825, the seventh child for Joseph and Abby Brown, in the small town of Henrietta, New York. The children in the large Brown family were free to express their beliefs. Growing up in the same household with a grandmother who was a committed Christian and who read Bible stories and paid attention to her grandchildren's religious education, Nettie felt inner stirrings about God even as a very young child. She looked forward to Sunday mornings at the Congregational church down in the village.

As Liberal Congregationalists they were taught that God is a friendly presence. Her parents and her church affirmed a God of mercy and goodness, not the punishing vengeful God of many orthodox churches. Instead, Liberal Congregationalists stressed God's understanding and forgiveness. They encouraged human initiative and goodness.

The thirty years following the new nation's birth were unsettling times for Americans who were searching for their own religion, their own spirituality. Many New England churches still clung to the Puritan attitude of severe punishment in this life and the next for disobedience to God's will—or to His church. The western frontier of the United States enticed folks to what seemed new and fresh as the New World had beckoned others two hundred years earlier. It summoned many who were stifled by religious orthodoxy. They could establish their own churches following a loving God and one to whom they could relate in their quest to live a good and prosperous but also self-determined life.

In 1819, Joseph and Abby Brown and their four children came to this new land of promise from Connecticut. Many transplanted Yankees were drawn to upstate New York's fertile fields near the Mohawk River. Joseph Brown bought one hundred acres of farmland with a two-room cabin near Rochester. His brother, a physician, lived nearby. The Erie Canal opened in 1825 and commerce extended trade routes to the frontier states. Life was good here.

Antoinette Brown was "delighted to steal away alone and lie on the grass or leaves looking up at the blue sky, or in the evening at the moon or the stars as they came out one after another," Elizabeth Cazden has written. Antoinette's spirituality was maturing in the serenity of the family farm.

"It seemed as though I had found a new heaven and a new earth," Antoinette reflected later in a personal journal. When her grandmother died, that event, rather than embittering her, "seemed to confirm her faith in a kindly God."

With the white ribbon pinned inside her collar, Nettie decided it was time to join the church. A few days before her ninth birthday, she answered the minister's call to come forward at the end of the service for all who wanted to join the church. At first, the members of the church had some misgivings about admitting Nettie to membership. She was a nine-year-old girl. As she spoke to them, they saw her zeal. They heard her convincing words. They voted unanimously to admit her.

Education at age thirteen was at the Monroe County Academy with two older siblings. Her distaste for housework and the encouragement from her parents propelled her to successfully pursue writing, teaching and preaching. Many teenage girls and boys found work as teachers after their short time in high school. Education was affordable to families of means. They could hire young single adults as teachers for their children, and for a short while, Nettie was one of them.

At the same time, inventions were being patented virtually overnight. The spinning wheel was replaced by a mechanical spinning jenny. Before long, store-bought goods manufactured in the textile mills replaced homespun cloth. The manner of housework improved. Things were changing all around Antoinette. She envisioned herself as part of the changing society. Young single women could find their places in religious activities and social reform work. However, no women were being ordained in the ministry. Even the Society of Friends, the Quakers, was admonished for allowing women to give public speeches. It was deemed "un-Christian and unladylike" for women to speak outside of their church worship services.

Antoinette, on the other hand, felt the call early in her teens. Cazden states, "Her brother William reported that on one occasion she gathered the girls in her classroom in a cloakroom and told them how pleasant it was to love and serve the Lord, offering a 'tender and touching prayer' that left the girls in tears." She took "for granted that God's call was not limited by gender."

Several options were open to Antoinette and other women of her day who were interested in serving in a religious capacity—

become a foreign missionary, marry a minister and be a help-mate to him, or remain a teacher in Sunday school. None of this appealed to her. She was determined to become a minister in her own right. She needed a theological education at a college, but most colleges didn't even admit women. There was one, however, in the area that would. Oberlin Collegiate Institute offered theology, but resisted Antoinette's application to theology classes because she was a woman. It was only after the assistance of other adults who supported her desire to enroll that the College Board finally admitted her. The preacher Charles Grandison Finney, an old family friend, was now at Oberlin as professor of theology, pastor of the church, and spiritual leader of the community. He became her mentor.

Both faculty and her fellow students constantly reminded Antoinette that the Bible did not approve of women speaking in church. The zeal and determination she exhibited as a nine-year-old carried her through the ordeal of writing an exegesis of Corinthians 14:34. This essay was published in the *Oberlin Quarterly Review*. She claimed that, in asking women to be silent in church, St. Paul meant only to warn against excesses in public worship. In the same issue, a professor rebutted her article and defined women's rights and duties more conservatively. However, the professor's patriarchal attitude of keeping women at home, in their place—the traditional chauvinistic view—did not deter her from her goal.

Seventeen years after pinning on the white ribbon, Antoinette, little "Nettie," completed her theological studies. Her goal of a theological degree was denied her until Oberlin finally awarded her an honorary Doctor of Divinity degree in 1908. The Congregational Church denomination initially denied her a license to preach because she was a woman. A year later they relented and permitted her to preach, although her ordination as a minister was withheld.

The decades of the 1830's through the 1850's witnessed the beginnings of the anti-slavery movement, the temperance movement, and the push for women's rights—especially the right to vote. Many would-be preachers were engaged to speak on theological subjects at churches. Antoinette Brown was one of the Oberlin students who bravely sought speaking engagements and thereby espoused her viewpoints on these social issues.

During one of her speaking tours in central New York State, the Congregational Church at South Butler, New York asked her to be their pastor. It was the moment she had been waiting for: her first ministerial position with a congregation, every Sunday. She was paid only $300 a year because the church was a poor rural parish.

Nevertheless, her enthusiasm overflowed. Cazden says in *Antoinette Brown Blackwell, A Biography* that Antoinette wrote to a friend, "The pastoral labors at S. Butler suit me even better than I expected & my heart is full of hope." She had many good women friends but most of them did not approve of women trying to break into a career that had long been dominated by men. The distancing of her dear friends later played a significant role when the enthusiasm of the pastoral duties turned to challenges for which she was unprepared and these challenges began to weigh her down.

In the spring of 1853, the South Butler church decided to ordain her as their pastor. Pastoral leadership, too, had been a formidable challenge and was a hard-won achievement. Before she became the first American woman to be ordained by a congregation, men first had to approve and bear witness to her capabilities. The Congregational Church was more orthodox than the liberal Unitarian churches associated with men like Samuel J. May and William Ellery Channing. Her exposure to liberal theological thinking at Oberlin College freed "little Nettie" more than she realized.

Cazden wrote that May and Channing were concerned that their liberal theological beliefs would cause questions concerning Antoinette's commitment to the Congregational Church. Men who had been her mentors and supporters did not attend her ordination. However, a Methodist minister friend was permitted to ordain Antoinette Brown on September 15, 1853.

Antoinette ministered to the South Butler church while continuing to attend conventions for the abolition of slavery, the temperance movement, and women's rights. She was a powerful speaker and earned the wrath of many protesters for her liberated attitudes toward women's rights. At the Women's Rights Convention of 1853, she and other women were heckled. Little Nettie maintained her courage despite the verbal abuse and threats of personal harm. She was, in fact, energized by the challenge.

However, an incident occurred within her first year as minister that contributed to her resigning her pastoral duties with the church. Two infants died before they were baptized. One was an illegitimate child whose mother's sin was considered to be the cause of the infant's death. At their funeral she could not bear to condemn those little souls to eternal damnation. It caused her such grief and pain that she was forced to withdraw from her pastoral contract. Coupled with the lack of support from her women friends, Antoinette suffered from depression and returned home to Henrietta. She felt as though she had failed in her calling.

This period of introspection was important to Antoinette's spiritual growth. It challenged her belief in a kindly God who had, nevertheless, taken her loving grandmother. She believed that her grandmother was with God. With the death of the two infants, who had no long experiences with life and no opportunity to learn about a loving God, Antoinette was forced to confront religious dogma she couldn't defend because she didn't believe it to be the ultimate truth.

After several months she returned to the lecture circuit and supported her friends in the women's rights movement. Laurie Carter Noble wrote in her biography of Olympia Brown, a woman student who was no relation to Antoinette, that Olympia invited Antoinette to speak at Oberlin College. Olympia had this to say on hearing Antoinette speak:

"It was the first time I had heard a woman preach and the sense of victory lifted me up. I felt as though the Kingdom of Heaven were at hand."

Olympia's enthusiasm to be a minister was as genuine as Antoinette's. They became friends, and Antoinette supported Olympia in her quest. She pinned a little white ribbon under Olympia's collar. After considerable challenges to her determination to become a minister because she was a woman, Olympia Brown became the first woman to be ordained a minister by a full denomination, the Universalists, in 1863.

In 1858 Antoinette Brown married Samuel Blackwell and together they had seven children. Samuel supported her advocacy and writings for the rights of women and egalitarian marriages. He took care of the house and the children when she attended and spoke at conventions. She was a prolific writer and lecturer.

The same year she became a Unitarian minister, 1908, Antoinette founded a church. She kept her faith in a loving God who supported the efforts of all humans to reach their potential.

The little girl, who once wore a little white ribbon pinned to her collar and challenged the customs of her time in order to become an ordained minister, lived long enough to vote in 1920. Antoinette Brown Blackwell died in November of 1921 at the age of ninety-six having lead Americans in both the nineteenth and twentieth centuries to the firm conviction that, in the eyes of God, all men—and women—are created equal.

Bibliography:

Antoinette Brown Blackwell. Macdonald, JoAnn M. The Unitarian Universalist Association, Unitarian Universalist Historical Society, Dictionary of Unitarian Universalist Biography, 2003.

Antoinette Brown Blackwell, A Biography. Cazden, Elizabeth. The Feminist Press, Old Westbury, New York, 1983.

Olympia Brown. Noble, Laurie Carter. The Unitarian Universalist Association, Unitarian Universalist Historical Society, Dictionary of Unitarian Universalist Biography, 2000.

Antoinette Brown Blackwell persevered to find a path to her vocation. She was fortunate in finding her mission in life at an early age and through a pivotal moment—hearing Reveend Finney's sermon.

Spike in "Gentlemen, Start Your Engines" discovers his calling through a key event in his childhood as well. Spike's inspiration is not the soft voice of an inspired minister but the deep-throated roar of a '36 Ford. He's not so transformed by visions of a pew-filled brick church as by visions of a crowded Brickyard. Spike's ambition is not to become an evangelist but an artist and an engineer. As you'll see, his exploration is just as beset by travail as Antoinette's but he, too, perseveres—even if he takes a much sharper turn toward artist than engineer.

GENTLEMEN: START YOUR ENGINES

by

Lucille Maurice Maistros

(Excerpt from *Growing up Colder: It Takes a Village Idiot*
© 2005)

One of our neighbors, Leon Piste, raced his black '36 Ford at the *St. Froid International Speedway* on Saturday nights in the summer. The gravel-surfaced track, about ten miles out of town, was only an eighth of a mile long, which made the sides so steep it was like driving around the inside of a mixing bowl. It was *International* because a couple of Canadians came down from Beebe, Quebec on the weekends to race, their cars loaded down with cases of Molson's beer and cartons of Export "A" cigarettes.

We had never actually been to the races, but we often sat under the lilac bushes on sticky summer nights and watched Mr. Piste in his driveway as he gunned that engine—va*rooooom, brom, brom, brom*—before he drove it up onto the trailer. Every Saturday night, from May until October. When we asked my father how come we never got to go to the races, he said he didn't see why we had to pay to go to the races when we could listen to that damn motor for free.

Ricky took himself there one year, when he was eleven, unbeknownst to my father. He bummed a ride with Leon's wife, Mabel, who was driving her own '47 Chevy in the Powder Puff Derby that night. Ricky, thrilled with finally being there, made himself at home on the gray, weather-bleached wooden slabs of the viewing stands and guzzled Coke from a ten-ounce glass bottle as the race started. Round the track they went, Mabel in second place for the first ten laps. She was closing in on Geraldine White's '55 Ford, hugging that slippery slope along the backstretch, when she lost control in the sharp-angled turn, flipped the car and catapulted end-over-end off the track and out of sight.

Ricky sat there, hotdog half-way to his opened mouth, as his ride home disappeared over the back turn.

After hanging around in the dust near the refreshment stand for about an hour, Ricky eventually found someone else to hitch a ride home with, but he was more concerned about Mabel who, although she would survive, spent the remainder of the racing season in traction at St. Froid General.

In June of 1959, nine-year-old Spike decided he was going to build himself a custom, one-of-a-kind go-cart. We called them go carts even though they were really soapbox racers with power only supplied by the steep hills of St. Froid. In a black and white photo taken that summer, Spike sits in his cart, his arm resting proudly on the open "window" ledge, a Purina Mills cap perched on the back of his head. Ricky along with two of the Voisin boys stand behind the go-cart, aimed like a rocket down the incline of our driveway toward Mountain Avenue, the most unique go-cart in the history of our neighborhood.

All the boys were building go-carts that year, three pieces of lumber nailed together in the shape of a capital "I" with four wheels taken from a wagon or baby carriage. A rope tied to each end of the front "axle" provided steering with the help of feet propped against the two-by-four to give a quick response "push me, pull me." No brakes—the driver would just drag his feet to stop, unless his leg snapped off.

Spike, however, was creative—an artist in the bud. We shared a similar approach to crafting a project, Spike and I; in my case, building a dollhouse: it had to be perfect in every detail. His go cart would have a cab, a windshield, a roof and a door.

Spike and Ricky set out to assemble what was needed to build his dream car, but they knew they couldn't ask my father for many building materials. Careful to a fault with his tools and supplies, my father was not the kind of man to hand out nails and screws like chewing gum. Between the double impact of The Great Depression and World War II, his conservatism was understandable. But Spike was a nine-year-old boy on a mission.

So, with his hand wrapped around the wooden handle of Dad's claw hammer, Spike plucked all the nails he needed from the clapboards on the side of our house, trying not to take too many from any one board so that it would fall off. It was a wonder our house didn't look like Mr.Voleur's, a man who worked with my father at Saxon's and who also drove a delivery truck for St. Froid Building and Lumber Supply on weekends. His house was a patchwork of brown cedar shake shingles and multi-colored aluminum siding salvaged from items that had "fallen off the truck," as I had overheard him tell my father. Dad had politely declined his generous offers of obtaining some really good building materials at really good prices.

Patiently, Spike assembled the other things he needed from various sources in the neighborhood. About some things, like the hinges for his door, I didn't dare ask for the source.

The top of his cart was soft, like a convertible. The door was hinged so it would open and close and a rope looped through two holes in the front axle for steering. He nailed a sturdy piece of wood to the chassis as a brake that swiveled on a nail near his left hand. All he had to do was pull back on the stick and it would hit the ground and stop the car...at least that was the idea. The only thing left to do was to take it for a test drive.

Spike's test drive was on a cool but sunny Saturday afternoon. While we'd sat watching *Gene Autrey and the Phantom Empire* that morning—our favorite adventure serial program—we had decided it was best to do it when Dad wasn't around. On Saturdays, he worked at his part-time job at the Volkswagen dealer. Saturdays were busy for Mom, too. While Spike prepared for his test drive, we could hear the moan of the Filter Queen as she vacuumed the living room.

Kids lined both sides of the street as Spike pushed the cart up the hill so he could give it a good start. When he got to the top, Red and Bobby Voisin held it steady while Spike opened the door and climbed aboard. I can see him now: holding the steering rope, adjusting his cap and telling Red to let'er go.

Spike hunched his butt and pitched his shoulders forward. The cart moved forward about an inch or so, and then stopped. Nothing. Oh, it rolled forward a little, like a skittish horse, while Spike grappled with the steering rope and pushed off with his feet. It was apparent that with all those extra features that he had built into it, Spike's masterpiece was design-saturated and speed-challenged. This Cadillac of carts was too heavy to roll.

Still, all the kids were impressed. Even when we pushed it back into the driveway, they gathered around to get a good look at it. It was cool. There wasn't another one like it in the whole neighborhood, and—for Spike's artistic nature—that was enough.

Although he didn't realize it before he started, Spike's journey of self-discovery wouldn't require wheels. When one's vehicular Mona Lisa looks so good standing still, there's no need for speed...or even motion!

Adam in "The Sorrel Mules" <u>does</u> need wheels—wagon wheels—for his journey. In the end, he may not know what career he'll pursue but he will find out something just as valuable. Adam discovers what kind of man he will become, what values and morals will determine his life's choices.

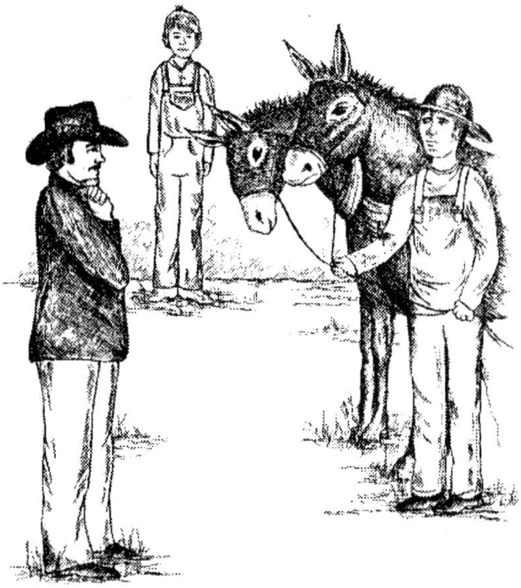

THE SORREL MULES

by

Ann M. Cook

Bits of chaff floated in the motionless air. Adam stabbed the pitchfork into the mound of hay, wiped his sweat-streaked face and blindly staggered in the direction of the door. The chaff burned his eyes and clogged his nose, making work in the loft intolerable.

Shoving the door wide, he balanced precariously in the opening while he gulped fresh air and rubbed his eyes. When his vision cleared he squinted against the hazy sunlight, scanning the empty sky for signs of rain. He watched the two milk cows lazily roam the drought-browned pasture, searching for vegetation. Before turning to the semidarkness of the loft he saw a swirl of dust approaching from far down the valley.

"That fellow must be crazy. He shouldn't run those horses in this heat. He's going to kill them," he said aloud.

It wasn't until the horses turned into the lane leading to the farm that Adam identified the buggy.

Brilliant red seats and colorful yellow-spoke wheels were his Uncle Dewey's trademarks of a profitable livery and horse trading business. The buggy was well-known throughout all of Crawford County and beyond.

"Yahoo!...Uncle Dewey!" Adam yelled, waving his arms in recognition. His reddened face beamed as he climbed from the loft and raced to the house. The Bantam chickens dusting themselves in the roadway flapped their wings and squawked in protest as he ran through their midst. He was at the gate when the buckboard came lurching up the hill, the frenzied horses lunging in the traces.

Dewey Goode stood spread-legged in the buggy, furiously tugging on the lines. He fought the crazed horses to a stop.

"Hey boy! How do you like this team?" he yelled.

The horses crouched with haunches quivering, eyes white-rimmed, dark coats stained even darker by sweat. Flecks of bloody foam dappled their broad chests.

"Where did you get them horses? They sure look mean," Adam said.

"They come from Wyoming, I'm told they're mustangs. Got me some good horses in this shipment. They look wild, but they'll calm down in a couple of days...make a real flashy team. My favorite sister here?" Dewey asked. He gasped for breath as he eased his bulk from the dangerously tilted buggy. He slid the ever-present pint bottle under the seat.

"Ma's inside. Pa's not here, he's over at the neighbors." Adam watched his uncle tie the lines to the fence.

"Reckon that'll hold them? What if they take a notion to run off?" Adam asked.

"I reckon it'll hold...they'll settle down; it's too hot to carry on so."

Dewey pulled tobacco and paper from his pocket and carefully rolled a cigarette. He took care to twist the ends into tight corkscrews before putting the match to it. Inhaling deeply, he pulled tent-size khaki pants up and started up the walk, motioning Adam to walk beside him.

"What you gonna do with those horses? You gonna try sellin' them to Pa?" Adam said.

"No need to worry about that. I plan on keepin' that pair. I always wanted a matched team of drivin' horses," Dewey said.

Sara held the screen door ajar while she surveyed her brother. A thoughtful expression furrowed her brow—she knew a visit from Dewey meant he wanted something.

"He never changes...still drinks too much and smokes too much," she murmured, noting the exaggerated color of his face and the extended purple veins in his too-large nose.

Dewey wheezed as he climbed the steps, pulling the white Stetson from his head to wipe rivulets of perspiration that trickled from his thinning hair into the tight collar of his white shirt. Sara opened the door and Dewey pushed past her into the cool interior of the house.

"Lord, but it's hot," he panted. He pulled at his tie and fanned himself with the hat.

"Come on in the kitchen, I've got work to do," Sara said.

Dewey and Adam followed along the dim hallway into the kitchen where several pots bubbled and gurgled atop a glowing cook stove. Sara stirred the contents of each pot before turning from the heat.

"Been a long time, Dewey. You don't come around much."

"Yeah, I guess it's been a while. I've been busy."

"How you doing? And how's Mae?" Sara asked.

"We're fine. Mae don't do much except stay home and tend to business. The reason I'm here now is that we want to take Adam to the fair, if it's okay with you and Charles," Dewey said.

He looked across the table where Adam sat silently. "That is, if he wants to go," he added.

"Please Ma, please let me go," Adam squealed, springing from the chair.

"I'll have to think about it. Meantime, you've got chores to do, so scat."

"Please Ma. Please." Adam pushed back the chair and fled to the door where he stopped to implore once more. "Please Ma, please, I'll get the chores done."

"Come on Sara, let him go." Dewey winked at Adam, his watery blue eyes disappearing into the heavy flesh under pale wiry eyebrows.

Sara paused, looking first at her brother and then her son.

"We'll ask your Pa. Now go get those chores done, or you'll not go anywhere."

Adam let the door slam, and through the window Sara watched him dash across the road. The chickens scattered before him only to come together again in his wake.

"I can't believe it's time for the state fair; is it starting early this year? Sarah asked.

"Only about a week, the summer's flew by, hasn't it?"

"How long you plan to stay?" Sarah asked, turning to Dewey.

"I figure about three or four days, till I get rid of the stock."

"Those crow-baits you call horses? I can't believe you're going to sell those horses to folk we know," Sara said in disbelief.

"How come you say that! I'm in the business of trading horses, whether it be to strangers or kinfolk. Of course, kinfolk always get the best deal," Dewey said, grinning.

"Nobody in their right mind ought to buy stock from you. You won't admit it, but there's something wrong with every horse you own."

"Now Sara. I buy in good faith and sell in good faith. I don't know any more about my animals than what I'm told. I can't tell if they've been doctored. Honest."

"Well then, how come you're always bringing horses in from places most folk never heard of?"

"I make better deals. Besides, with feed being scarce, most farmers are selling off extra stock."

"Yes, stock that's not worth keeping. Then you sell them to our neighbors."

"I have to sell while they're still in fair condition. An animal can eat an awful lot."

"Brother or no, it's a good thing I don't know what's wrong with those horses. If I did I couldn't stand by and let you fool people the way you do."

Sara went to the icebox and returned with a pitcher of butter-milk. She poured a glass and handed it to Dewey.

"You'll have to make do with this...I've nothing else to offer," she said, seeing him eye the buttermilk with distaste.

"This is fine. At least it's cool."

"If we let Adam go, you have to promise you won't learn him any of your tricky ways."

"What tricky ways?"

"You know what ways," Sara said.

"I don't know what you're talkin' about, but I promise." Dewey raised his right hand and placed it over his heart.

"Me and Mae wouldn't lead the boy wrong, you know that Sara."

"Don't try to tell me that. I know different, and for some reason Adam thinks you do no wrong. Course being only fourteen, he's easily impressed," Sara said.

"Well, what do you know. I didn't know the boy felt that way. He could do worse...there's a good living to be made dealing horses."

"Charles and I are trying to bring him up so he'll do right by his fellow man. He doesn't need any lessons from you."

"Come on Sara, I don't do intentional harm to anyone. If

they buy, it's their own doing, not mine."

"You figure the time you sold that wind-broke mare to Jim Hall hasn't been talked about? It's embarrassing to us when we hear folk talking like they do."

"Honest, Sara, I never knew that mare had the heaves," Dewey said, his right hand again covering his heart.

"You take advantage of people... I see it all the time. I don't want Adam to think that's the way to do."

"A man's got to make a living, what with the depression, and now the drought. It's costly feeding stock and not being able to sell at a good price."

"Just hear what I tell you. I don't want Adam learning bad ways. When are you going?" Sara said.

"Tomorrow. It'll take near five hours and I have to stop by the old Farley place."

"I heard some family moved onto the place. Are they living in the old house? I heard it's falling down. I hope they're not paying rent."

"I don't know about that. They must be in a bad way. He's got a team of mules to sell—needs the cash. I sent word I'd take a look at them. Might be able to help him out."

"More than likely you'll be the one that makes out the best."

Dewey grunted to his feet and went to the kitchen door. He patted each vest pocket before finding a fresh, neatly folded square that he used to dab his face.

"How do you stand it in here?" he said, shoving the wet handkerchief in his back pocket.

"I try not to think about how hot it is," Sara answered.

"Guess I'll be on my way. Better not leave those horses too long. If you figure Adam will be going say so and we'll come get him, if not, we'll just go on."

"I ought to ask Charles before I say Adam can go. He should be home soon, but he'll probably say it's okay. He always does."

Sarah stirred the contents of the pots and moved them to the back of the stove. She fussed with the handles of each, trying to delay an answer. She searched for a logical reason why Adam shouldn't go, but found none.

"He can go. He probably won't sleep all night thinking

about it, so whenever you get here he'll be ready."

"Swell. Mae will be mighty pleased. She likes kids. Too bad she never had any," Dewey said. He took his hat and followed Sara through the dark hallway.

"See you in the morning," he called as he climbed into the buggy and snapped the reins over the backs of the horses.

From the calf barn Adam saw the horses leap forward, throwing Dewey off balance and nearly causing him to tumble from the buggy. He saw his uncle grapple with the lines trying to gain control of the bolting horses. As the runaway team plunged down the hill, Adam was sure he saw Dewey give him the thumbs-up sign.

Adam slept fitfully and at first light was up and dressed. At the familiar sounds of the cook stove being stoked he hurriedly stuffed a pair of overalls and shirt into a small box and dashed downstairs.

"Uncle Dewey won't forget me, will he Ma?"

"I hardly think so. Give them time, it's barely light."

Adam went to the screendoor, straining to see in the weak light.

"Ma. Is Uncle Dewey an honest man?" Adam asked.

Sarah turned from the stove. "Why do you ask?" she said.

"Some of the kids say he isn't real honest. I don't believe them. Uncle Dewey isn't dishonest, is he Ma?"

"I won't say he's bad, but sometimes I wish he would do things differently, especially some of the deals he makes selling those horses and mules."

"I've never seen him do anything wrong. I just wish the kids would stop talking like they do. It makes me feel bad...I like Uncle Dewey."

"I know. He likes you too."

The grinding of iron-shod wheels and the sound of horses reached his ears long before he saw the procession. Over the clamor Adam heard cursing as his uncle tried to keep order among the kicking, biting horses tied to the back of the heavily loaded wagon. They stopped just outside the gate.

"Come on boy, let's go," Dewey yelled.

Adam tossed the box on top of the clutter and pulled himself up and over the side. He squeezed in next to the silent

Aunt Mae as Dewey bawled at the team, setting the entire train in motion.

Halfway down the hill Adam looked back and waved.

"Bye Ma, bye Pa," he called, gesturing furiously from the cramped quarters.

Dewey angled the wagon and assemblage of horses onto the main country road and a slap of the reins settled the wagon team into a fast walk.

"The Lord must be mighty displeased with us, or else He'd send some rain," Mae said, indicating the dry creek-bed nearby. She brushed at the gray coating of dust that settled on her dress and cast her gaze toward heaven. Dewey looked at her and started to comment, then shook his head and stared over the backs of the horses.

The shrill horn and sudden appearance of an automobile from behind sent the horses into a snorting, bucking, swarm of confusion. Dewey cursed loudly as he struggled to bring the team to a halt.

The automobile came to an abrupt stop. "Get out of the way," the driver shouted.

In an attempt to escape the evil-sounding machine, the terrified horses reared and pawed sending up swirls of dust that obscured the driver's vision.

"Get out of the way! You've no right to block the road!"

He put the automobile in reverse and backed away from the stifling cloud.

Dewey made no effort to clear more than half the road.

"Damn, no-good automobile...never will amount to anything."

Dewey glared at the driver as the automobile bounced over the rough edge of the road.

"Poor man never can afford one. Only thing they're good for is noise and flat tires. Besides that, they scare you to death," he snorted. He pulled the team to the center of the road as the car disappeared behind a cloud of dust.

"Pa says that one day everybody will be driving one," Adam said.

Dewey slapped the reins across the backs of the horses, inducing them to increase their pace.

"Your Pa is wrong, dead wrong. Horses and mules always have been and always will be…those danged mechanical things are too flimsy for hard work," he said sharply. He snapped the reins again, urging the horses into a trot.

Adam glanced at Mae, but she was studying the worn pages of her Bible. He looked at his high-top shoes and tried to think of something to say. He didn't like Dewey being mad. He wished he had not mentioned what his Pa thought.

"Aunt Mae, look…there's a pheasant." Adam pointed to the cock bird that scurried into the underbrush.

His attempt at conversation went unnoticed, for Mae remained straight-backed, still squinting at the Bible's fine print. She traced each line with an arthritic index finger, her mouth moving soundlessly. As Adam tried again to think of something to say, Dewey touched him lightly on the leg.

"Okay, boy, this is where we turn off. Keep your eye on them horses and yell if they give any trouble."

Dewey swung the team onto a narrow rutted lane that curved away from the main road to wind between the arid hills of the highlands. The usual green carpet of grass was chewed to the roots by foraging cattle, and the hills stretched brown and lifeless into the distance.

The house huddled amidst a grove of dead locust trees. Traces of white paint clung to the underside of the eaves, but now, except for the buckling red-brick chimney, the house was a nondescript gray.

Dewey pulled the horses to a stop just outside the barren yard as a horde of children appeared. Shaggy haired, clad in grimy bib-overalls, their shoulders and arms tanned and lean, five boys straddled the decaying porch railing swinging their dirt crusted feet.

Four thin-legged girls, with dresses all the same red polka-dot, stood near the door and gazed from beneath heavy sun-streaked bangs.

From amid a cluster of crumbling outbuildings a scarecrow figure appeared and motioned Dewey to the far end. As the wagon started moving the boys ran to the edge of the yard as if to follow, but stopped when the man looked in their direction.

To Adam, the farmer looked older than his probable age.

His weathered, deeply lined face and stooped shoulders made him look more like a grandfather to the young children.

"You Mr. Goode?" he asked.

"That's right. Hear you got some mules to sell."

"They're at pasture. I'll bring them," the farmer said. He touched the brim of his hat as he walked away

Adam compared the man's shoes with their worn heels and loose soles to the shiny new boots his Uncle Dewey wore. It seemed this whole family was hungry and threadbare.

In a short time the farmer returned leading a proud pair of horse mules, blonde sorrels, with flaxen manes and tails. At sixteen hands, and apparently well fed, they dwarfed the small man who held the halter ropes.

Dewey's eyes widened, then he smiled, rubbed his palms together and climbed from the wagon. He hiked up his pants, pulled the Stetson down to his eyebrows and circled the mules, eyeing them intensely. He grunted occasionally, then his nicotine stained fingers paused at the slightly enlarged hock of the off mule.

"Look's like he's spavined," he said.

"Don't bother him none. Goes just as good as the other," the farmer said. He patted the animal's smooth flank.

"Give you fifty dollars a-piece," Dewey said.

The farmer's jaw sagged and he stepped back in surprise.

"Fifty dollars! These mules are worth three times that much, maybe more. They're young, good for at least twelve, fifteen year," he said.

"Fifty is all. Take it or not," Dewey said. He turned toward the wagon, pausing to pull tobacco from his pocket.

"Wait…wait. Let me think for a minute."

"Okay, but I don't have time to quibble," Dewey said.

The farmer shifted from foot to foot. Several times he looked at Dewey, then at the mules, his brow furrowed.

"You won't have any trouble finding a buyer for mules like these. They're fancy…every farmer I know wants them," the owner argued.

"Look man. See that string of horses. I'll be lucky if I sell half of them. Nobody has any money, including me."

"Yeah, but there's always a market for mules. They're better at pullin' a plow than horses. You stand to make more when you do find a buyer."

"If you figure you can do better, go ahead and sell them yourself," Dewey said.

"Lord knows I've tried. There isn't anyone around here with any money. They all want my mules, but they can't pay."

"Then what's to say I can sell them?"

"You have more chance...I don't know where to find a buyer."

"Well then, I guess you either sell for what I offer, or else you don't sell at all," Dewey said. He tapped tobacco into the thin paper trough and carefully sealed the ends before putting the cigarette to his lips.

"Okay, I'll take the fifty. I need the money...bad."

Dewey reached into his pocket and drew out a wad of bills. He counted the money twice before placing it in the farmer's outstretched hand. The man handed the leads to Dewey and wearily turned toward the house where a woman stood in the yard surrounded by the children.

Dewey led the mules to the wagon, his ruddy faced screwed up against the smoke curling along his cheek. He winked at Adam.

"Okay boy...let's get these mules hitched up."

Adam jumped to the ground and unhitched the horses, tying them with the others. With a few adjustments, the mules were in the harness and moved out easily with the loaded wagon. As they passed the house Adam looked for the children, but the porch and yard were deserted and he guessed they were told to stay inside until the visitors were gone.

The usually crowded fairgrounds were almost empty. Only half the corrals were occupied by steers. They, it seemed to Dewey, needed a steady diet of corn and hay. With so few people, Dewey and his uncle quickly found a suitable place under a big oak tree to set up camp. Despite the drought, there was enough grass and water to last four or five days.

Most of the fair-goers knew Dewey by sight and were eager to inspect his animals, especially the sorrel mules.

When the campsite was set to Mae's satisfaction, she started the fire and began preparing the evening meal.

"Go fetch some water," Mae commanded, noting the

lowering sun. "Got to have water to cook with...don't want your mama sayin' I didn't feed you."

"Ma knows you won't let me go hungry," Adam said, pulling two water buckets from the wagon's jumble of goods.

"Can't never tell. Some folk are strange," Mae muttered, directing him toward the pump.

"Yes ma'am," Adam said.

Dewey had unhitched the mules and gave each a generous ration of grain. He tethered the horses and then stepped back to admire his purchase. The speculative trance was broken when Adam walked up.

"Uncle Dewey, Aunt Mae said supper's ready."

"Okay boy. Be there directly," Dewey said, tying the mules in the choicest grass.

"Soon as we eat I want you to curry them mules," Dewey mumbled.

"Mae, you and me can get the dress harness ready...there's still time to trot out before dark."

It was near sundown when they finished the meager meal. "How'd you like them beans? I grew them myself. Had to teach Mae how to cook beans. She didn't know how to cook beans, never uses enough fatback," Dewey said.

"That was a good supper," Adam said.

"A body has to eat, whether they like it or not," Mae quipped over her shoulder, as she started toward the wagon.

"Don't pay any mind to Mae, she isn't herself. Must be feeling poorly," Dewey said. He reached for the ever present pint bottle and took a sip.

"I won't," Adam said.

Dewey and Mae polished the harness while Adam curried the mules.

"Ain't they fine mules?" Dewey asked, winking at Adam.

"They sure are," Adam replied. He wished the farmer could see how grand the mules looked in the nickel-studded harness.

"Come on boy. Let's trot out. We want to stir up interest in these mules...just walk slow and let folk take a look."

They circled the fairgrounds, but nowhere did they see moneyed men. Those present were barely getting by and in no position to pay the amount Dewey knew his mules could bring.

They only offered comments about the mules, and Dewey, in return, managed to turn their interest toward his string of horses.

"How much for that chestnut gelding?" a prospective buyer asked.

"That's a fine animal. No vices, and he's sound. Let you have him for twenty-five dollars," Dewey said, making no mention of the horse being unbroken.

"Whew! That's way out of my reach…can't afford more than ten for any horse," the man said.

"Okay. If that's all you have, he's yours. You got yourself a fine animal," Dewey said, clasping the man's hand and shaking it vigorously.

Adam wondered if the man was aware that his newly purchased horse was untamed. He also wondered if the man really wanted to buy a horse. He was sure his mother would not approve of her brother's selling tactics.

By the third day most of the horses were sold, but still no one talked real money for the sorrel mules.

Dewey and Adam were hunkered at the campfire when a nattily attired man appeared.

"Uncle Dewey, some fellow's interested in the mules."

"Well…well. I think I have me a buyer." Dewey slid a bottle into a back pocket. He strode to where the man, dressed in split-tail jacket and bow-tie, stood gazing at the mules.

"Howdy mister," Dewey drawled. He pushed back his hat and hooked his thumbs over the silver belt buckle.

"You have a splendid team of mules," the gray-haired man said. His speech had none of the local dialect and Dewey took him to be one of the 'Grand Englishmen' who were buying up property for the Union Cattle Company.

"These mules are prime stock. They're the best. You never go wrong buying prime stock," Dewey said.

"I am in the market for good work stock and am willing to pay top dollar," the Englishman said.

"Is that right? It looks like we're both out of luck."

"How's that? Are the mules not for sale?"

Dewey squeezed his eyes shut and the corners of his mouth drooped.

"I can't sell these mules…they belonged to my Pa. I promised him I'd never sell his mules," Dewey moaned.

"Is your father here?" the man asked.

"No. He passed away, near two months ago. Pa raised these mules, made me promise I'd never sell his mules," Dewey said. He drew a handkerchief from his pocket and dabbed at his eyes.

The gray-haired man strode back and forth. "I surely would like to buy this team," he said.

"I swear. I promised Pa I wouldn't sell his mules." Dewey patted his hip pocket and pulled out the half-pint flask. He removed the cap and offered it to the would-be buyer.

Without hesitation he took the bottle and, with the deftness of a long-time drinker, swigged most of the liquor in one gulp. He smacked his lips and rubbed the top of the bottle against his sleeve before returning it.

"Sure would like to have those mules. How much is a team like that worth?" he asked, his gaze frozen on the bottle.

"At least four hundred dollars. I could get more; sorrel mules is first prize," Dewey said. He again presented the flask.

"I'll give you three hundred for them," the gray-haired man said, eagerly taking the offering.

"I see you're a man who appreciates good drink. Got just what you need," Dewey said. He went to the wagon and extracted a quart Mason jar.

"This is the best 'white lightning' around," he announced, seeing his prospect's face flush with anticipation.

Sunlight streamed through the clear liquid, making a kaleidoscope of pattern on the man's face.

The gentleman's hand trembled as he took the jar and hastily removed the top, some of the contents sloshing over the lip. He downed the hard liquor, barely stopping for breath between swills.

"Will you accept my offer?" he said, wiping his mouth.

"I swear to God, I can't sell those mules," Dewey cried, directing the words toward the campfire where Adam and Aunt Mae waited. He folded his hands and turned his face toward heaven.

Adam did not want to be involved in the sale and was glad when Aunt Mae rose and hurried to where Dewey stood. She grabbed his arm with a birdlike grip.

"Dewey, you can't sell your Pa's mules. You promised.

On his deathbed you promised. I heard you, I heard you. If you sell those mules the devil will get you; he'll get you for sure."

Dewey shrugged her off.

"Dewey, you'll go to hell if you sell those mules…you'll burn in hell," she shrieked, threatening him with a crooked forefinger.

Dewey shook her off and she hurried back to the fire, clasping the Bible to her breast. She rocked back and forth as she stared at the flames, mumbling to herself.

"I'll raise my offer to four hundred and fifty," the man said. He grabbed at one of the mules for support.

Dewey winked toward Adam as he grasped the man's limp hand.

"I reckon Pa will have to forgive me for selling his mules. Leastways, I'll pray he will," he said. He dried his eyes and made out the bill of sale.

Adam watched the gray-haired man pay his money and stagger away, the mules plodding behind. He hoped the new owner would be as proud of the mules when he sobered up as he was now.

"Come here boy," Dewey ordered. He drew Adam to his side and draped his heavy arm around the thin shoulders. "Boy, you've got to realize I'm in this to make money. Maybe it's best if you forget you ever saw them sorrel mules. Hear?"

Adam looked at his Uncle Dewey. He did not know this man. For the first time he saw a bulbous-nosed, unethical liar who took advantage of the weak and the unwise. It was against everything his Ma and Pa were teaching him, and Aunt Mae even helped with his deception.

Adam had to admit the kids at school were right; Uncle Dewey was not the man Adam thought he was.

Adam had misplaced his faith in his uncle but the mistake is hardly fatal. In fact, Adam spiritually profits from his experience. We come to believe at the end of "The Sorrel Mules" that Adam is much more likely to be like his honest and industrious parents than his deceptive aunt and uncle.

With "Hunter" by Danny Imwold, we continue biblical names for the protagonists and a moral lesson through the outcome. We also have another instance of misplaced trust. Jacob trusts a man whose life he saves. Jacob's lesson in trust, however, may prove to be his <u>last</u> lesson.

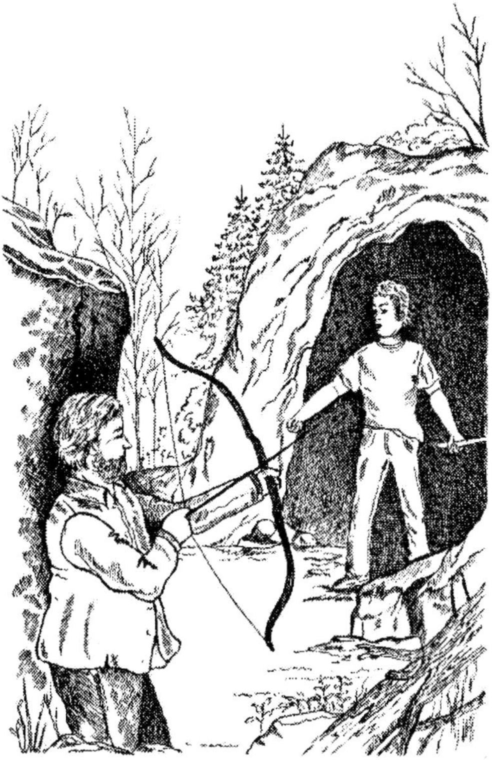

HUNTER

by

Danny L. Imwold

The arrow was twenty-four inches long, its shaft having once been part of his favorite birch tree. The feathers at its end had come from a dead owl he'd found along one of the paths he used regularly. The business end was a razor sharp point that he weighted using bits of metal cut and honed from bits of metal debris found along the roadway. And the arrow flew straight and true.

With only a whisper, the shaved wooden projectile twisted slowly on its mission, its trajectory not more than one inch above the arc from its launch point. The line to his quarry was, except for a few browned leaves, clear and open. And the point of the small missile found its mark, the steel cutting flesh, the shaft losing six of its inches in the chest of a Whitetail doe.

Jacob Masery had lived the last twelve of his twenty-seven years as a recluse. He'd learned the arts of camouflage during his early years as a boy scout, learned how to hunt and fish from his grandfather who'd raised him until his thirteenth birthday. When Grandpa died, Jacob had packed as many things as he could carry and walked off into the woods. He hadn't looked back.

Spending his first few winters sequestered on Spencer Island in the middle of the Susquehanna River, just opposite the town of Port Deposit, he learned very quickly how to keep warm, the importance of keeping clean, and the greater importance of being invisible to other people. When he did cross the river into town for necessities, he did nothing to draw attention to himself, walked with his head turned to the ground, and spoke only rarely. Money came from selling bait to the fishing shops along the river or from scavenging recyclable items for payment. He never asked for handouts.

Few people actually ventured onto Spencer Island, even during the warmer months when fishing would preoccupy many sportsmen. Jacob watched from the banks of Spencer, humoring himself with the preoccupation of fishermen and their newest lures, equipment or techniques. He'd never had any problems with his line and pole, but it was fun to watch. And he learned a lot. About people. Interactions.

When he was eighteen, he used a small boat he'd rescued from the trees along the shore and moved to Garrett Island, in the middle of the Susquehanna between the towns of Perryville and Havre de Grace. With a larger space, he was able to develop shelter on a high point in the center of the island where he could see visitors approach from some distance.

Deer were few, unless he swam over to the north or south shores of the river, but other game was plentiful. This doe, however, had swum the shorter distance from the north shore and was feeding lazily on the grasses that lined a small meadow on the island. And Jacob had tracked her.

He pulled the carcass into the air against a beech tree at the edge of the meadow and slowly opened her with his knife. He always hated this part, this draining of life from one of God's creatures. But he had no choice. He firmly believed that God had left man in charge of the earth, and that His other creatures were here to serve man in whatever capacity they could serve. This one was food.

When he finished, he stored the meat away and stood at the opening of his home in the rocks in the early dusk gazing toward the highway bridge that spanned the river. Lots of traffic. He liked to watch the vehicles moving in opposite directions across the bridge, wondering what each of the occupants was thinking as he or she drove either into the sun or away from it.

A large truck, emblazoned with the words "QUALITY MEATS" moved across the span following closely on the rear of a smaller box truck with undecipherable words printed on its sides. As Jacob watched, the first truck began to smoke at the wheels. The "QUALITY MEATS" trailer continued to move toward the forward truck and in an instant the two collided amidst a gnashing of metal and hammering of steel. Together they filled all the lanes of traffic and began to push one another toward the wall separating them from the long fall to the river. Then the smaller truck broke through the wall.

Jacob held his breath as the cab of the first truck exploded through the concrete and steel retainer and hung precipitously for moments above the water, then pulled itself through the opening and plunged into the waters of the Susquehanna. The twisted cab of "QUALITY MEATS" clung to the broken edge of the bridge.

Jacob didn't stop to think. Racing down the path leading to the river's edge, he began pulling off his shirt and shoes, his bare feet mushrooming puffs of dust from the dry dirt trail as he ran to the water's edge. The truck had entered the river waters less than one hundred feet from where the path dropped into the river and Jacob swam several strokes before the chill of the water began to counteract his adrenaline.

The south-flowing current moved him quickly to where the truck had entered the water and he could see lights just below the surface.

He dove down into the murk, swimming for those lights until he touched metal. He could feel the side-view mirror as he pushed for the door and felt the grip of the handle seconds later. Jacob pulled on the handle but the pressure from the surrounding waters held the door firm. Swimming across the front windshield he felt for the passenger side window and found it partially open. He reached in and wound the window down further, then, his lungs beginning to burn, pulled himself inside the cab.

Rising to the driver's side of the interior he found a small pocket of air and inhaled deeply, his chin just above the water. Reaching through the frigid blackness he felt for any forms inside the truck. There was a hand, a forearm connected to a shoulder which led to the slumped form of the driver. Jacob pulled at the body but could not move it. Seatbelt. He reached in and began feeling for the seatbelt catch.

His thumb depressed the button holding the belt snug and the driver's body went limp inside the cab. Gently Jacob pulled him from the truck and pushed for the surface.

Gasping for breath and still holding onto the driver of the truck, Jacob began swimming for the shore of his island. Struggling desperately to keep the man's head above water, he swam hard against the current toward the embankment. Finally, nearing exhaustion, Jacob Masury pulled his unconscious burden from the water.

Together they lay face down in the mud of the Susquehanna, motionless. Finally, Jacob pulled himself up, reached over, and lifted the driver's head. The man coughed.

"You okay?" Jacob asked.

More coughing and sputtering.

"Hey!" Jacob shouted to the man lying next to him, "can you hear me?"

The other man groaned, spat water and bile, and murmured, "Yes." Slowly, they crawled through the mud until they were on dry land. The driver again fell silent.

Jacob pulled the man, who appeared to be in his mid-forties (some gray in his hair and a bit of a paunch at his belt) up onto the path and beneath the branches of a scrub pine. He lay there catching his breath and staring back at the bridge where traffic had come to a standstill amid flashing red and blue lights. A helicopter was making its way up river, its search beam already reflecting off the water, and two fast moving boats were cutting across from the Havre de Grace shoreline.

Jacob looked again at the man lying next to him. Though still, the man was breathing evenly and Jacob was certain he'd be okay. Looking to the boats in the water again, he decided he'd better make his way back to his hideaway before someone saw him.

He found his shirt and shoes a little further up the path and put both on in an attempt to fend off the cold that had begun to work its way into his body. There was too much activity now around the island for a fire; he would simply have to curl up under his blankets to keep warm. By the time he reached the hideaway, it was nearly dark, and he could see beams of light penetrating the water where the truck had belly flopped onto the surface. No one had yet approached the island, but that would soon change. He crawled in and tried to sleep.

Sometime during the night he heard a boat's motor and voices, one shouting something that made Jacob believe the driver had been found. The *thup-thup-thup* of the helicopter circling overhead was so loud that Jacob was forced to cover his ears with his hands. An hour later the glow of lights and the sound of the boats finally faded, leaving him with the peace of mind that no one had come looking for him.

He woke early the next morning feeling somewhat chilled but otherwise happy with himself. Emerging from the shelter into the early sunshine, he walked over to the rocky crest of the hill and scanned the river. A barge floated over the place where the truck had gone in, the wreck already on its platform, water flowing in small streams from its doors. Police blocked traffic on the damaged bridge, rerouting cars to the other span while work crews began repairs to the broken wall.

All that day and into the next, Jacob remained hidden, avoiding the boats and police that continued to hover around the site of the accident. After nearly three days, things seemed to return to normal and he decided it was safe to go into the town for needed supplies.

He finished a cold breakfast, then walked down to a small cove thirty feet directly below his hideaway where he had an old wooden boat tied under some overhanging trees. He set off across the channel rowing as quickly as he could, then beaching the craft on a small mud flat on the opposite shore and tying it to a tree.

He hiked the short distance into the village and walked into one of the convenience stores fronting the highway. He picked up a few things that he saw as luxuries—toothpaste, toilet paper, salt, pepper—and walked up to the counter to pay. Not wanting to look into the face of the clerk, he glanced down at a stack of newspapers in a nearby rack. The headline caught his attention. TWO BODIES FOUND IN TRUCK IN RIVER.

"Oh my god," he whispered to himself. He added a paper to his other purchases, paid and read as he walked slowly across the parking lot. He stopped at the nearest bench and slumped down to read. "How could I have missed them?" he asked himself. "I let them drown." A tear formed at the corner of his eye as he read.

The bodies were those of two Pennsylvania college students who'd been missing for two days, but they hadn't drowned. The girls had been found in the rear compartment of the truck, each with multiple stab wounds to the stomach and upper torso The police had not found the driver of the vehicle and assumed that he had drowned and floated away. The search now took them further downriver, and they expected the driver's body to drift ashore some distance south. A picture of the driver was next to that of the two young women. He was in his mid-forties, salt and pepper hair, heavy-set build. He was the very man Jacob had rescued. He was also wanted for the kidnapping and murder of a third student in Delaware.

Jacob put the paper down and sat for a moment. Then, leaving the groceries on the bench, he began running toward the river. He found the boat and pushed it back into the water, jumped in, and rowed quickly back to the cove. Making his way up the trail, he suddenly stopped and crouched next to a tall pine. "He's still here," he thought to himself. He focused on the surrounding trees and shrubs, scanning for movement, and trying to remember what the man had been wearing.

He always carried a penknife, but the blade wasn't very long, would not prove to me much of a weapon. He'd have to get back to his shelter, find something more lethal or at least threatening, and find the killer.

He began slowly climbing the path to the top of the hill, moving as quietly as he could. Reaching the granite slabs at the top, he slowly edged his way across the surface, peering over the edge toward the hideaway. Nothing. There was no movement inside the inner circle or at the shelter; nothing looked as if it had been disturbed. He slid down the rock face and ran the short distance to the shelter, lifted the camouflage cover and stepped inside.

His eyes adjusted quickly to the dim light and he looked around, spending several seconds scrutinizing the shadows in the recesses of the cave. It seemed empty. He lifted the cover at the top that allowed more light into the shelter and walked over to a ⸱recess he thought of as his closet. He reached in and removed a walking stick with a sheathed hunting knife slung at its end and felt for his quiver of arrows. It wasn't there.

A tinge of fear began to raise the hair at his neck as he turned and scoured the enclosure looking for the bow and arrows. He threw back his blankets, checked through the wood pile, but they weren't there.

"I must have left them outside," he mumbled under his breath.

He pushed through the cover and broke into the sunlight, and stopped cold. A drawn arrow, its shiny tip sparkling in the brightness, was pointed at his chest. He'd pulled this man holding the bow from the water three days before, and now that same man was standing only eight feet away, perhaps ready to kill him. His beard had grown out and his clothes were filthy, but he looked healthy and well fed.

"I been watchin' you. You do pretty good here. Nobody even knows you're here, do they boy?"

Jacob held the sheathed hunting knife and the walking stick in his left hand, staring at the man holding the bow, and wondered how he could somehow regain control.

The killer glanced at Jacob's left hand, drew tighter on the bowstring, and said, "Don't get brave, boy. Drop 'em." Jacob had no alternative but to do as he was told. He dropped the two weapons to the dirt at his feet.

Trying to delay the man from releasing the arrow, Jacob squinted and said, "The police think you're dead."

"Yeah, I figured that." He loosened his pull on the bow string slightly. "How long you been hidin' here?"

Jacob thought about that for a second. "I'm not hiding here," he responded, "my buddies and I come up here every spring and camp out for the weekend," he lied. "I just came up a few days early."

The man pulled the bow taut again. "Bullshit! You're laid out here for a long time. Anybody can see that. I figure I can hide here for a while myself. Now, where's the rest of your food?"

Jacob watched the man carefully, saw his arm twitching from holding the bow taut, knew that he might release the razor-sharp arrow momentarily. The way the man held the bow with the arrow tilted down slightly at the notch and the way his elbow bent inward at its shaft, Jacob feared the killer might release even without meaning to. Now or never, he thought. He lunged at the man.

The bowstring straightened with a *thwung* sound, scraping the man's forearm and peeling off layers of skin. The arrow flew off the bow in a wobble, slicing just below the skin of Jacob's left arm then spiraling off into the trees. Jacob kept moving, tackling the man at the waist and driving him back into the rocks behind them. Blood spurted from the gash in his forearm as he pushed up from the man and tried to pull away, but the killer wrapped his hand around the wound and squeezed hard. The two stumbled back into the clearing.

Backstepping quickly, Jacob tripped over a tree root and together they fell to the ground, the killer on top. Jacob threw his right arm hard into the man and the two began to roll back to the crest of the rocks. They stopped at the edge, the man holding Jacob down with one hand and reaching for a rock with the other. Without thinking, Jacob pulled the man tight to his body and rolled over the rock edge. For several seconds they dropped through the air toward the cove where the boat was hidden.

They crashed through the trees and shrubs along the cove's edge and plunged into the cold river. Pinned beneath the man in four feet of water, Jacob clung tightly to his foe. He could feel the man thrashing on top of him, trying to reach the surface.

Rolling the man like an alligator drowning a doe, Jacob was able to push his head above water and gulp air. His hands found the killer's shoulders. He pushed hard and his muscles tensed against the desperate thrashing of his attacker. He held the man under the water. Long moments later, the man finally stopped moving. Jacob released his grip and pulled himself up onto the muddy bank.

That evening, Jacob Masury floated the man's body to the middle of the Susquehanna River where he'd first pulled him from the water. He released him. Funny, he thought, somehow there's some justice in this. The strong current carried the partially submerged body south toward the bay.

Six days later, a newspaper article declared that, "the body of a man believed to be the fugitive driver of a truck that had sunk below the bridge across the Susquehanna was recovered yesterday by Aberdeen police. The man, identified as Ronald Gary Olsen, a convicted murderer from New Jersey, is believed to have murdered three women before the truck he had stolen was run off the bridge during a freak accident involving another vehicle. Olsen was apparently injured in the accident and drowned."

Jacob Masury dropped the newspaper into a nearby trash can and headed back to the now peaceful river.

We now move from the eastern portion of Maryland to the western end. Just as the placid Susquehanna River and the pleasant island retreat of the reclusive Jacob played a part in "Hunter," the cold, the wildlife, and the beautiful wilderness of Garrett County are admired and enjoyed by the real-life members of the Deep Creek Rod and Gun Club.

In Frank Soul's nonfiction history of close friends and relatives, we see men whose outdoor skills and enjoyment of nature are as important to them as they are to the fictional Jacob. Unlike Jacob, they don't depend on hunting to survive. Rather, they depend on each other and a balance with nature for the survival of a way of life and the unsettled beauty of a piece of Maryland.

THE DEEP CREEK ROD AND GUN CLUB: BEGINNING OF A DREAM

by

Frank Soul

(Excerpts printed with permission)

Chapter 1 My first deer hunt in the mountains

*"A dream is just a dream.
A goal is a dream with a plan."*

Once upon a very long time ago, I took my first hunting trip. In 1960 my brother, Harry Gilbert, was kind enough to take me deer hunting in Western Maryland. I was only twelve years old and I thought this was the greatest epic undertaking that could happen to a kid—this hanging out with his big brother and his buddies and hunting deer up in the big woods. Harry told me stories about how he had hunted up on Piney Mountain since 1952 and the great times they had camping out, almost freezing to death hunting in the snow, and even (once in a while) harvesting a deer, and boy, I couldn't wait to try it!

The first time we went, Harry's buddy, Marlin Taylor, drove our whole group. Marlin (should have been a good omen: he must have been named after a make of hunting rifle!) borrowed an old furniture truck from some friend. This puffer and clunker was an old 1950's-era Ford that had a metal roof on the back bed and canvas sides. It was home for us for about four or five days. By the way, it's two hundred thirty miles up to Piney Mountain from our home in Harford County, and it took us nearly ten hours to get there—and that was with only one stop to get a bite to eat and coffee to go. This was before Wal-Mart could take an hour to do what it only took ten minutes to do in 1960. Our rickety Ford covered wagon strained at forty-five miles per hour on level ground and barely beat a walking pace going up hill. After what seemed like an eternity to get to Piney Mountain, we fell out and stretched like unused accordions. We got our camp set up and it was great; however, by the time we got everything done it was dark and these so-called buddies of mine told me stories all the way up the road about good things and bad things about Piney Mountain. The one story that struck fear in me instantly was about all the bears on the mountain and how they liked to eat people. Needless to say, they made me go to the spring to get water for cooking, making coffee, and washing.

However, the whole gang needed an hour of nagging and pushing to persuade me to go after the bucket of water with a flashlight so dim you had to strike a match to see if it was lit.

The spring was only about twenty yards from the truck and I was so scared that you probably couldn't stick a toothpick up my butt. As I was getting this bucket of water out of the spring, Marlin crept through the bushes and let out a big roar! In a slice of a second, I leapt higher than a buck, turned faster than a rabbit, and buzz-sawed my legs through briar and bramble as fast as...well, as fast as I ever moved in my life. The water went flying, the bucket got launched, and, as far as I can tell, is still orbiting around our good earth like a Sputnik. The next time I got water, I made sure the sun was shining, camp was close, and I made enough racket to wake Lewis and Clarke!

Chapter 8 Harry's sausage gravy

I remember one day Harry was going to make sausage gravy for breakfast for himself, Charlie, and me.

I think this was the first time that he ever attempted to make gravy because the more he added flour and stirred it, the thicker it got. I'm not sure he knew gravy's not supposed to be cut into squares and eaten like brownies. He added scoop after scoop of flour until it was so thick that the spoon wouldn't move anymore. What we had was one big glob of sausage surprise.

The two of us held a conference and, despite the fact that we could barely boil water successfully ourselves, decided that he put too much flour in the skillet. Two cups of flour is just a little too much for a ten-inch skillet of gravy. We had eggs instead. Harry put the skillet of sausage surprise outside in the cabinet. We cut chunks out of it the rest of the day and, after thinning them down with some milk, we had our sausage gravy.

We ended up having sausage gravy all week from one skillet-full. About the third day, we finally got the spoon out of it. Somebody could've had a gravysicle, I suppose, but by the third day, the novelty must've worn off.

Chapter 14 The beginning of our dream

Bum told me that he had a small piece of property that he would sell us if we were interested in building a cabin and starting a hunting club in Garrett County. After a little time, Harry, Charlie, and I started talking and our fantasy became a dream, took a left turn into a nightmare for a time (just kidding), and finally became a reality we still enjoy now.

We had a few get-togethers, shot nothing more ambitious than bull, and finally started our club. Since the property was near Deep Creek Lake, we unanimously agreed to name it "The Deep Creek Rod and Gun Club." Our membership consisted of Harry Gilbert, Charles Bunker, Ed Knill, Ted Liller, Jim Liller, and me. We added a few more as time went by—Don Longfellow, Frank Rather, Frank Simmons, Arch Kerns, and Bob Orr.

We looked like a cross section of loggers, pirates, mountain men, and hardened hillbillies and we were a group to be reckoned with. Still, we were only so tough because of the wilderness we cared about—not because we were naturally ornery. Well, maybe a few of us were naturally ornery. After the required number of tall tales had been told and ridiculed, we officially started our club on January 26, 1975.

Chapter 15 Camping in the blizzard

We made our last camping trip to hunt in tents and my old jeep truck on Piney Mountain during the 1974 deer season. We hunted the first day, which was Saturday, and we all went to bed Saturday night as it started to snow. By daybreak, there were two or three inches of snow on the ground and then the mountain's clouds got down to serious business.

Ted, Jim, my son Brian, and Jim's son Jimmy left to go home Sunday morning only to be stopped in Grantsville (still smack in the middle of the Garrett County high country) because the roads were closed. The Grantsville Fire Department brought everyone who was stranded back to the firehouse by snowmobile to enjoy each other's company for a few days. We faired pretty well up on Piney Mountain in my old jeep camper and at Bum's cabin; however, my tents were destroyed. It never stopped snowing until Wednesday—four days straight of moderate and heavy snow—and we ended up with forty-two inches of pure beauty and highway-hiding blanket.

We finally got out and got home by the next weekend. They extended the deer season that year because I think all the deer got on a bus and went to Florida for the winter—nobody saw much of hide or whitetail as far as I could tell. We didn't get to come back to hunt again that year but maybe it was just as well. If a twelve-point buck lowered his head to find a bit of leaf or grass, you probably couldn't have seen him!

The cold of a Maryland winter in the mountains of Garrett County can surprise and alarm a first time visitor. Keyser's Ridge often sees temperatures below zero and thick snow blown sideways by a wind that called Canada home only hours before. Those who ski, hunt, snowmobile, hike, and icefish better have enough layers to look like the Michelin man if they expect to survive.

But there's another sort of cold, that sometimes surrounding the human heart. The snow in the next tale is only a light dusting but the cold calculations of a killer's intent are much more dangerous.

A LIGHT DUSTING OF SNOW

by

Mary Beth Creighton

The young girl was covered with a light dusting of snow, an eerie shroud glistening in the low rays of the setting sun. Lying on a cold slab of granite high on the ledge known as Hammer Rock, the supine figure was the unseen goal for the determined group hustling through the brush and creek-bed below.

Detective Adam Carson and the three deputies from the Cosgrove Sheriffs Department sweated and cursed as they crunched across the half-frozen earth.

The snowstorm the night before had left a blanket of six inches across the county. Earlier, the sun had melted the snow into slush. Now the temperature was falling. The sky filled with flurries and put a light dusting of snow atop the crusting slush. If the weather got too bad, the rescue chopper wouldn't be able to fly even if they did find her alive.

"Shit!" Adam cursed as his right foot slipped on the freezing mush. He threw his arms out and managed to straighten his leg out without losing stride. Agile and determined—a track star in high school—he was a good hundred yards in front of his colleagues. He coughed with the effort; he was still dealing with the aftermath of the chest cold he had caught from his three-and-a half-year-old daughter Hailey. Still he pushed on and was the first to arrive at the rock face.

Ignoring the hot fingers of muscle ache stabbing his side, he started up eighty feet of jagged cliff. He couldn't spare the time for safety lines, but there were still spikes from the climbers back in autumn. Hammer Rock was a popular climbing spot in every season except winter.

Dear Jesus, let him get there on time! Focus, he told himself. Stay focused. Don't panic. But he let his mind wander to that morning when he'd played in the snow with Hailey. His wife had suited her up head to toe in bib-overalls, boots, gloves, hat, and fuzzy scarf. She had looked liked a stuffed puff-a-lump—her pudgy cheeks rosy from the chilled wind.

They had made snow angels and gone sleigh riding. He could still hear Hailey's giggles as the toboggan raced down their back hill. "Let's go again Daddy!"

It was surreal, Adam thought. He bent his knee and placed his foot on an outcropping of rock—surreal to go from such joy and contentment to a horrifying life and death race against time. His face slick with snow and sweat, he pushed on up the cliff. He heard his team hammering in additional climbing spikes below. Spider-like, he crept higher and higher, determined to save her.

Suddenly Red shouted his name. He flinched. It saved his life. The bullet whizzed past his ear before he heard the crack of a rifle. It ricocheted off the stone. Luckily it deflected away from his face. Gunshots erupted in return. Heart beating violently, he struggled to reach his Smith and Wesson, gripping with his feet and left hand.

There was movement in the woods to their right, but the figure was already a shadow in retreat. Johnson and Bedard headed after it, Red laying down cover fire.

"You okay Carson?" Red shouted, her voice panicky.

Adam's fingers slipped off his still-holstered gun and he reached up to touch his stinging right ear. He lowered his head and saw blood on his finger. Just a nick.

"I'm okay!" he yelled back.

He clawed for a new handhold and started up again reaching with his right foot towards another crevice. Slipping off the freezing rock, he dangled by his hands for a torturous second. He grunted and cursed and groped quickly for a new foothold.

Angry, frantic, and flying on adrenaline, he scaled the last fifteen feet recklessly. He pulled himself over the edge and saw her. She was just a few feet away—still and angelic, a modern day sleeping beauty.

"Jesus Lord! Please," he begged, scrambling to her side. Trying to remain calm, he reached for her pale throat.

* * *

"Noooooooooooo!"

"Adam, wake up. Wake up!"

"She's dead. Oh, God...she's dead!" Adam said in a raw voice, his arms flailing.

"It's all right honey. It's all right now. It was just a dream," Beth said softly, wiping the sweat from his brow with the edge of her cotton nightgown.

"I'm okay." Adam slowly sat up and looked at his wife, "I'm sorry."

She was sympathetic, but frustrated. "Don't be sorry. Talk to the department psychologist. Please, Adam. You hardly get a good night's sleep anymore. And it's been worse after each woman you find. The one this week in the creek...."

"She was so beautiful, Beth, so serene. For a split second I thought she was alive, but it was my own pulse. Then for a moment I was relieved she was dead and thought, 'She's better off leaving the pain behind, the suffering.' Jesus, Beth! What kind of person does that make me?"

"A tired person." Beth patted his shoulder.

Adam shook his head and cleared his throat. "Cold and brittle, like a skeleton decaying in the ground."

Beth rose up on her knees. "Stop it! Stop talking like that. You're a good per...."

"He's letting each victim live longer now," he interrupted. "Letting us get closer—mice to cheese." He tossed back the quilt and climbed out of bed. He walked to a window and leaned against it, his head resting on a sweaty forearm. Outside was coal black—no moon, no light—just dark like his mood. "But we're just puppets and he's the puppet master; he sets the stage and controls all the moves."

He slumped against the window. He had a job to do and he did it, but there was always another body, more pain, more, grief, more suffering. How long could he keep trying to balance scales? How long could he face evil and still find the light afterwards?

"You're going to get him," Beth said. Her voice was soft but determined. "He thinks he's so clever, but he's going to make a mistake. Besides, he's underestimating you."

Adam almost smiled. Beth was his rock; her confidence was a gift considering all the crap she endured as a cop's wife. He turned to look at her. She was sitting back on her heels in the bed, hair tousled around her shoulders. She was so lovely. All golden haired with pretty pale-blue eyes set in the sweetest heart-shaped face he ever saw. Physically, he was the gloaming to her dawn—Sicilian olive skin and black curly hair.

Steadier now, he walked back to the bed and let Beth tug him down to sit beside her. Reaching out, he traced her cheek with his finger. She smiled and those blue eyes blinked back tears.

"Lay back down, sweetheart, and try to get a few more hours of sleep," she urged him.

"Okay. I'm just going to check in on Hailey first."

He padded down the hallway to Hailey's room. His precious daughter lay curled on her side, the Cinderella nightlight casting a glow on her small form.

Relieved to see Hailey looking peaceful, he quietly crept to her side and lightly kissed her cheek. He wouldn't tell Beth that in his nightmare, their daughter was the killer's victim. Before he awoke screaming, he had seen her lying dead on the ground, her skin translucent over delicate bones—looking pale and angelic.

He kissed her once again and said a silent prayer of thanks.

*　　　　*　　　　*

"Da Deeee!" Hailey called. "Wake up!"

Adam opened his eyes to squint at the digital clock on the nightstand. Seven. Beth was up, but the spot beside him was still warm. He stretched and climbed out of bed to shave and shower. Afterwards, he dressed in khaki slacks, shirt, and V-neck sweater, his usual working clothes. Finally, he unlocked the dresser, checked the load and safety of his gun, a Smith and Wesson semiauto, and holstered it in its harness. Walking down the steps, he smiled when he smelled coffee brewing and something baking.

"Good morning," Beth said cheerfully as he walked into the kitchen. She was standing at the counter pouring coffee, her wispy hair tucked behind her ears.

"Good morning. How're my girls?"

"We made cinmon rolls," Hailey told him proudly. She was sitting in her booster chair poking chubby fingers into the icing of the rolls on the table. She was also painting the icing on her face.

"I'm a lucky guy." Adam pulled out a chair and plopped down. He snagged a roll off the plate and took a giant bite. "Mmm...mmm."

"Daddy likes 'em, Mommy."

"Of course," said Beth bringing the mugs to the table. "His two best girls made them." She sat and looked at Adam, her left eyebrow arching slightly.

"Wha...?" Adam asked with a mouthful of roll.

"You look tired."

"Gee, thanks." Adam rubbed his chin. "I even shaved."

"No ants!" Hailey chirped.

"That's right, no ants."

"You can sleep in tomorrow," said Beth. "It's Saturday."

Adam washed down the bite of roll with some coffee and looked over Beth's shoulder at the buttercup wallpaper. The edge was peeling away from the windowpane. One of these days he'd get around to fixing it. One of these days.... "Thanks for breakfast, Hon."

"Adam."

He gave Beth a guilty look. "You know I can't rest until we get this guy."

"What guy Daddy?"

"Nobody Hailey," Adam said curtly. "Eat your breakfast."

Beth glared, but kept her tone mild. "It's supposed to snow tonight. Maybe you could manage to spend some time with your daughter tomorrow before you push yourself to exhaustion. It's been weeks of sixteen-hour days, Adam, and you're just getting over a cold. You can't possibly be at your best like this."

Adam held her scrutinizing gaze. "Beth, you know what this guy does."

"What guy Daddy?"

"Shhh!" Beth snapped this time at Hailey. "Oh!" Tears filled her eyes. "I'm sorry baby. Mommy and Daddy will talk about the guy later." She sniffed hard and pushed away from the table without eating.

"Aren't you hungry?" Adam asked.

"No. Come on, Hailey. Let's get you cleaned up for Granny. She's going to play with you today while mommy goes to work."

"Disney?" Hailey asked as she lifted sticky fingers toward Beth.

"Yes, mommy's going to the travel agency to work today. Maybe somebody will want to plan a trip to Disney." She scooped up Hailey and called over her shoulder coldly as she left the kitchen, "Have a good day."

"Yeah, right." Adam swallowed the last of his coffee and looked longingly and regretfully after his wife and daughter.

* * *

In the bullpen, Adam grunted a greeting to his colleagues and marched straight into Conference Room B. A map of Cosgrove and its surrounding counties dominated the far beige wall. Tacked to a corkboard to the right wall were the faces of six young women. All lovely, all blond, all dead.

Guilt suddenly struck him as he stared at the pictures. He hadn't been able to save any of them and it was eating at him, so badly, in fact, he'd snapped at his little girl. How much longer could Beth put up with his lack of presence, his lack of support?

He shook his head, disgusted. He was failing on all fronts. Forcing his mind back to the murders, he stared at the victims' faces. The murders had initially occurred a week apart but for the last two weeks the killer had escalated. Now he kidnapped and murdered unsuspecting females every four to five days. Adam's team had been working day and night to nail down the killer, dodging the press and the growing panic, criticism, and wild speculation.

"Who's going to be number seven?"

Adam turned. It was Libby Phillips. She'd been a police officer for the last five years, half as long as Adam. A transplant from Chicago before she started her police career, she was smart, fearless, and a knockout. Dressed to kill, she wore tight, stretch blue jeans and a black leather blazer over a skin-hugging turtleneck. Flaming red hair, though probably from a bottle, helped make her a bombshell and an object of careful second looks from some of her male colleagues.

"We're getting close Red, I smell it." Adam walked to the map tacked to one of the corkboards. "All the vics were taken within a fifty-mile radius of town." He tapped a pushpin marking the precinct. That's three counties. Here, Hayden, and Rossville. All the vics were found in Cosgrove, though." He gestured to six red pins scattered randomly around the blowup of the town.

"Why?" Red moved up behind him.

Adam could feel her breath on his neck. He shifted uncomfortably. "There are a lot of why's." He paused to cough and clear his throat of some morning congestion—and, maybe, relieve a little of his unease.

Red patted his back. "At least you don't sound like you're hacking up a lung anymore."

"Yeah," Adam agreed.

She put her hands on his shoulders and began to knead his muscles. "Jesus, you're stiff."

"I'm okay."

"Hold still and let me work out these kinks." She moved her long fingers nimbly across his shoulder blades, her thumbs rubbing circles at the base of his neck. He stood stiffly—tensing muscles, not relaxing them. "You know Adam, despite the circumstances I'm really glad to have the opportunity to work with you. I've been wanting to...."

"Hey! I want a turn," Hank Bedard shouted. He and Jake Johnson, the other half of the team, stepped into the room. They were working plainclothes for this case, like Red.

"Sure," agreed Red innocently, "Then it's my turn." Hank plopped into a chair and Red moved behind him and started to rub his shoulders.

Grateful for their timing, Adam turned back to the board. "Back to the why's," he continued. "Why these particular woman? Was it random or planned? Why the games with us? Is it the thrill of almost getting caught?"

"We had the last woman located within twenty-four hours of being taking," added Bedard. A veteran of the force for nearly twenty years, he preferred working in the field, preferred taking orders instead of giving them. With tanned skin, a lion's jaws and mane of dark hair, Bedard used his looks and an occasional growl to intimidate even the toughest perps. Only a growing waistline detracted from his king-of-the-grasslands image. "How much was great detective work, and how much was what the killer let us know?"

"A lot of friggin' questions," agreed Johnson. The junior deputy was only eighteen months in the field, still idealistic despite his somber tone. He sat on the conference table chewing gum and put his feet on a chair.

"Right there, Red," Bedard sighed. "Oooh, yeah...that's the spot. You're better than Ben Gay."

Red chuckled. A minute later she declared it was her turn and they switched positions.

Adam paced. "Let's take a ride out to the last dump site," he said finally. "Forensics hasn't found anything new, but I want to take a look again."

"You smell something, Boss?" asked Johnson.

"Maybe, kid, maybe."

* * *

They took Rosy. Rosy was Bedard's police-issue Ford. The divorced father of two grown boys, he had a long history of Rosies. His famous words were, "She's fast, smooth, and purrs likes a kitten—just like a woman ought to. And she don't talk back."

Adam sat up front with Bedard, Red in back with the kid. Let him deal with her pheromones for a bit. He thought of Red's increasing flirtations. When this case was over, he was going to have to have a long talk with her.

Twenty minutes later, they reached the creek where they had found Janice Fitzgerald posed on the bank under a covered bridge. She looked white and serene, a Sleeping Beauty waiting only for a kiss. The only signs of violence were the red marks around her wrists and ankles. The COD was the same—death by an overdose of injected narcotics. Morphine or Dilaudid had been found in each victim's blood stream. The coroner estimated that Fitzgerald had died from an overdose of Dilaudid only an hour or two before Adam and Red found her.

An anonymous phone call led them to her. They raced to the location, but once again, it was too late. The woman was dead. Young, pretty, and about to move to Florida, she ended up on a cold stream bank instead of sun-heated sand.

"Carson, you still here?" asked Red. They were standing at the edge of the water, Rosy parked on the bridge above. "Carson?"

"I'm here," he answered, and gently shrugged her hand from his wrist. He glanced over at Bedard and the kid squatting by the water, but they didn't seem to notice. "Just thinking, Red."

"Go on."

Adam tucked his hands in the pockets of his parka and glanced at the spot Fitzgerald had been found. "The timing is too perfect, the coordination too precise. He's not working alone."

Red looked surprised. "Could be."

"It makes sense. It's unusual for a serial killer, but think about it. All the women were taken from parking lots. It was either early or late. People shop at all hours nowadays. Still, no one remembers seeing anything. A few times there was a distraction—the fire in the dumpster at Wal-Mart, the lost child at the grand opening of the Tons of Fun Play Center. The women are just walking to their car and bam! A vehicle pulls up and they disappear. Much easier if you have a driver and a grabber, not to mention a watcher."

"Three people?"

"I don't know." Adam turned his head to cough. "Maybe it's an initiation of some kind."

"A gang?" Johnson asked as he stepped over. He sneezed suddenly and pulled a crumpled tissue from his coat to wipe his nose.

"Better put a hat over your cue-ball head," Red teased. "I think you caught Adam's cold."

"Hey! I like my buzz."

Red smiled, but her tone turned serious again. "It doesn't play like a gang. The ground's too frozen for tracks, but there's been no sign of multiple perps around each scene—no bunches of broken twigs, cigarette butts, nothing."

"Gangs deal in drugs," Johnson suggested. "The vics were drugged."

"Yeah, but these killings aren't a money thing or a status thing. What we got is classic serial killer."

"Red's right," Bedard said from behind him. He held up his hand. Something thin dangled from his gloved grasp.

"Fishing line. Found it trapped in some rocks about ten yards down stream."

"Could be somebody was fishing," Red said.

"Could be what our perp used to tie up the vics," Adam suggested. He pulled out a clear evidence bag from inside his parka and Bedard slipped it inside. "Let's get this to the lab."

"Yeah," said Bedard, shivering. "It's too damn cold out here. He pulled off his wet gloves and started up the hill, but then paused. "Here, kid," he said tossing a set of keys at Johnson. "You're younger and faster. Get up there and warm the car up."

Red laughed and started behind them. "You coming, Carson?"

Adam nodded and took one more look at the spot Sleeping Beauty Janice Fitzgerald had been carefully laid before he turned away.

* * *

Adam got home and rolled into bed just after one. The lab guy, Tubby, had assessed that the fishing line was consistent with the ligature marks on the victims' wrists and ankles. The brand of line was so common at area stores, the clue, if it <u>was</u> one, was practically useless.

Adam's hunch about the parking lot distractions caused the team to call back the store managers and workers at the abduction sites to question them further. Several incidents, possible distractions, were discerned—a couple fighting, an accident nearby, an angry customer. They couldn't come up with any names but a police report had been filed regarding the accident—a hit and run a block away from a grocery store where one of the women had been snagged.

Adam questioned the driver of the rear-ended Impala. He was an old man who used his annoyance at being bothered to vent. "Goddamn drivers these days think they own the road. The weasel took off like a jackrabbit and slammed into my car. He backs up his souped up menace to society and races off without a care in the world."

Other than a description of the car—which the cops never found—the conversation hadn't been helpful. One fact played around in Adam's head though. The Mustang that hit the Impala didn't have any tags. The old man was sure of it.

Adam drifted off thinking that the killer was not only clever, he had resources.

He woke up bouncing.

Hailey was beyond excitement pointing out the window at the snow that had fallen overnight. Bouncing on the bed she chanted, "Let's play in the know Daddy! Let's play in the know!" "Know" was currently how she pronounced "snow."

Adam rubbed his eyes and looked at Hailey. How could he resist his cherub-faced cutie? She had her mom's pale blue eyes and his dark curls—a combination that would have him interrogating every boy who wanted to date her. Pushing thoughts of work aside, he told Hailey to go get in her snow clothes. She cheered as she slid off the bed and skipped out of the room yelling for her mother.

Two cups of coffee and a bowl of Cheerios later, he threw on his winter gear and smiled at Beth as he took their Eskimo-clad daughter out to play in the snow. An hour and a half passed before they came back inside rosy cheeked and ready for hot chocolate.

Hailey was too wound up for a nap, but settled in front of the TV to watch cartoons while he and Beth folded laundry.

"I'm going to head in for a few hours, Hon. The plows have already been through and the temperature's rising."

"Okay." Beth stopped folding a Dora-the-Explorer pillowcase and looked at him. "Be careful." Her eyes implied concern beyond his driving in the snow.

"When this case is over, I'm going to take some vacation time. Maybe we should go on a trip. Do you know a good travel agent?"

"As a matter of fact, I do."

He smiled. "Okay, you plan the trip and I'll take the time off."

"You promise?"

"I double promise." He crossed his heart and blew her a kiss on the way outside.

*   *   *

Feeling lighter, Adam cleared the snow off their Jeep and slid behind the wheel. One of these days he was going to have a garage built. Despite the snow, the ride into work didn't take much longer than the usual fifteen minutes.

He'd told his team to take the day so he was alone in the conference room that morning. Glad for the solitude, he read the files again—every entry, every report. Pieces of the madman's puzzle were still floating around in his head, but he felt they were starting to gravitate to a sensible orbit about the dark star of his killer. Maybe today they would fall into place.

Beth called him before noon and said her mother was coming over to watch Hailey. She was meeting one of her colleagues at the travel office for an urgent customer appointment. She wouldn't be too long.

By two o'clock his stomach was moaning for lunch. Outside was sunny and bright from the melting snow. The sidewalks were clear so he walked around the corner to the sub shop and got a loaded Italian sub. He was halfway back when his beeper went off. It was Dispatch.

He raced back to the station and up to the desk sergeant. "Sir, 911 Dispatch just got an anonymous call," the officer told him. "Caller claims another victim was kidnapped."

"Shit! When? Where?"

"The caller didn't say, and the call wasn't traceable."

"Lord…this guy doesn't even take a snow day. What else did the caller say?"

"That's all, sir."

"Okay, get my team in here. I want to know as soon as any additional information comes in."

"Yes, sir."

Still clutching his sub, he headed to his office to call home. He was thinking about Hailey and the nightmare. His mother-in-law answered the phone on the second ring. "Hi Joyce, everything all right? Is Hailey okay?"

"Hailey's fine, Adam. Why wouldn't she be?"

"No reason. What's she doing?"

"She's right here in the kitchen making a Playdough castle."

"That sounds like fun. Listen, Joyce, do me a favor. Make sure all the windows and doors are locked, okay?"

"What's going on Adam?"

"It's just a paranoid's precaution—this case has me feeling a little jumpy, that's all."

"Hmm. All right, I'll make sure the doors and windows are secure."

"Thanks, Joyce."

"Don't worry. Hailey and I are having a grand time."

"Okay, thanks." Adam disconnected with a strange feeling in his gut. Something wasn't right. Why had the killer called to brag about a kidnapping while not giving a location for the body like before?

He walked out to the desk sergeant. "Have we gotten any new missing persons reports?"

"No sir. Nothing in Cosgrove or the surrounding counties."

Adam walked back to the conference room to await his team. All the missing women had turned up within forty-eight hours or less of their kidnapping, all dead. In three of the cases they had been reported missing. Three others had turned up dead before anyone even knew they were missing. What was the connection? What was he missing?

He paced for ten minutes until Johnson and Bedard arrived. Frustrated, he told them what he did know. "The son-of-a-bitch will call and give us a location," he snapped, "when he knows it's too late for us to reach her in time."

"You're taking this personally, Boss," said Bedard.

"Damn right I am." Adam fired back. "We got women disappearing into thin air then overdosed with a controlled substance. We got no motive. Forensic information hasn't led us anywhere. I can't sit around here waiting for the killer to reel us in like perch."

"Let's go back over it," Bedard suggested. "Maybe we're talking a medical professional. Doctors and nurses have access to narcotics."

"Druggies steal shit all the time," Johnson said. He blew a bubble with his gum and popped it with a finger.

"True."

"Maybe the killer was jilted by a girlfriend and he's taking revenge on blondes that look like her."

"Maybe the perp is a jilted girlfriend."

Adam listened to Bedard and Johnson toss around theories, but his mind drifted to the new woman who had been kidnapped. Oh, he had no doubt someone was missing. Her friends and family just didn't know it yet. Whoever she was, she must be terrified—terrified and about to lose her life. The phone on the conference wall rang, snapping Adam back. He jogged over to pick it up. "Carson."

"Adam, it's Joyce."

Instantly, Adams muscles bunched into tight cords. He clutched the phone. "What's wrong? Is Hailey okay?"

"Hailey's fine. It just that...well, I'm just a little concerned about Beth."

"Beth?"

"Karen—you know Karen Moore who works with Beth—well, she called here looking for her. She said Beth never showed up at work. Beth took my Pathfinder since it has four-wheel drive. You don't think she had an accident do you?"

"I hope not. Joyce, you sit tight. Keep everything locked like I said before."

"Okay."

Adam hung up and quickly dialed the travel office.

"Hello. This is Karen at Vacations Forever. How may I help you?"

"Karen, it's Adam Carson. Did Beth get there yet?"

"No. And her client didn't show up either."

Adam took a breath for calm, noticed Johnson and Bedard standing by him now listening. "Karen, is there a Nissan Pathfinder in the parking lot?"

"Yeah, I saw one when I came in. I thought maybe it was the client's."

"Okay, listen carefully. You make sure all the doors are locked. I'm sending the police."

Holding back panic, he flew into the bullpen and laid out the situation. Johnson and Bedard were on his heels. Red, in faux-fur coat and boots, was climbing out of her Ford Bronco when they hurried out the door and down the front steps.

"What's going on?" she asked anxiously.

"I think he's got Beth!" Adam shouted.

"What? Oh no, oh God, no. Get in!" Red slid back behind the wheel and was peeling wheels before Adam had the door shut.

"Vacations Forever Travel Agency on Lindale and Main Streets."

"Beth's work?"

Adam nodded. "There's a small parking lot out back. There's a lawyer's office on one side and a Karate place on the other. I doubt they're open, but maybe we'll get lucky. Karen Moore is there. Beth was supposed to meet her there for a customer appointment."

Red slid into the parking lot behind the cruiser and they scrambled over to the Pathfinder. It was empty and locked. Inside the travel agency, Karen was crying in the waiting room. Before the tears she'd managed to pull up Beth's appointment calendar on the computer. "I called the number listed, but got no answer."

Adam just stared. Reality was starting to sink in.

"Send a uniform over to that address and look for one Reginald Lakes," Red ordered one of the officers. "And send some officers door to door here. The businesses on either side are probably closed, but something across the street may be open."

"Where's Beth?" Karen asked sniffing through tears. "What's happening?"

"We're trying to find out," Red said soothingly. "Officer, please take Ms. Moore to her office and get her a drink of water."

"Thanks, Red," Adam said gratefully after the officer escorted Karen away. "I'm off my stride here."

"No problem. Just take it easy." She took his hand. "You need to sit down too."

Adam shook his head and headed toward the door. Johnson and Bedard were outside by the Pathfinder. "You got the key?" Bedard asked him.

Adam shook his head and told him to go ahead and have the lock jimmied. He watched as a uniformed officer slipped a metal strip down the window seam. He tried to play the abduction through his head. Beth must have parked, gotten out, and locked the door. Someone pulled into the lot asking for directions, and Beth good-naturedly trotted over to help. She was likely pulled into the vehicle before she knew what happened.

Trying not to think about how scared she must be, Adam helped search the Pathfinder. They found nothing, not even Beth's purse. The snow had been plowed and the sun had melted any tracks that might have been made by another vehicle.

Damn! He hoped the uniforms going door to door came up with something, but he had a terrible feeling his wife had disappeared without a trace.

*　　　　　*　　　　　*

The first break came an hour later. The customer who was supposed to meet with Beth about a vacation turned up at his condo. Reggie Lakes, an openly-gay computer analyst with a good salary, seemed a reasonable vacation prospect.

"Look," he told Adam and Johnson in the interrogation room at the station. "I told you. I met this guy at Big Ron's bar two weeks ago, guy named Pepper."

"Pepper what?" Johnson asked.

"I don't know. He never said. Is he in trouble?" Lakes stroked nervously at his long brown ponytail. He was a pretty man, with strikingly high cheekbones and a smooth complexion. Tall and lean, he wore tight black jeans, fur lined snow boots, and a sweater that looked to be cashmere.

"So you met him at Ronnie's and…."

"We dance, we have some drinks, then we go back to my place. We share some weed, we climb into bed, we do the thing, then he leaves. The next week it's ditto. But this time he says how he's so burnt out. He needs a vacation. He asks if I like sex on the beach."

"So you agree to pay for a vacation just like that?"

"Well, yes…look, he's hot. So he tells me Beth Carson at Vacations Forever booked his friend's trip to St. Thomas. Pepper wants to go to St. Thomas too. So I make an appointment for next week to meet with this Carson lady, but Pepper calls this morning. He says some Amazon-sized accountant offered to take him to Cancun. Anyway, he's tempted to say yes and blow me off, but if I can show him the booking to St. Thomas, maybe he'll stick with me to rock and roll. He gives me Mrs. Carson's home number—says his friend gave it to him."

"So you called Mrs. Carson at home and asked her to meet today."

"I sort of told her I had to go out of town unexpectedly so I really needed to book the trip today."

"You lied."

Guilt flashed in his eyes momentarily. "Yes," he admitted. "Pepper naked on the beach. That's all I could think about. It's not a crime."

"Why didn't you show for the appointment?"

"Pepper called me back and said not to. He knew I was making an honest effort and it was wrong of him to give me an ultimatum like that. He said he would call the travel agency and reschedule for sometime next week when we both could be there."

"What time was that?"

"Around ten this morning I guess."

"Where does Pepper live?"

"I don't know. We never go to his place. He says it's a dive."

"Phone number?"

"No, he always calls me on my cell."

"Describe Pepper," Johnson ordered.

"Short black hair streaked with blue. Does his make-up like Cleopatra."

"Height? Weight?"

"Pepper's long and strong," Reggie said an expression of awe on his square face. "I'd say he's at least six feet four. I don't know about his weight, but he's busting with muscles, despite his habit."

"Habit?"

"Yeah, he likes his coke and ecstasy; says his friend keeps him stocked."

"What else did Pepper tell you about his friend?"

"He bitched about her. Said she's a little psycho, but she has good connections."

"Drug connections?"

"Maybe. He used to push to support his use, before she came along. Now he trades in favors with her."

"Did he mention her name?"

Reggie shook his head. "Is Pepper in some kind of trouble?" he asked again.

Bedard ignored him. "Where did Pepper meet this lady friend of his?"

"I don't know, but not here in Cosgrove from what I gather. Listen, can I go now, or are you gonna frisk me again?" Reggie smiled suggestively.

"Listen, Reggie boy, we're far from over."

Adam left the room and let Johnson do his thing. He was a good interrogator. Red handed him a cup of coffee outside the door. "Thanks."

"I'm so sorry Adam."

They walked to Conference Room B and stared at the boards. "All the women have been found in Cosgrove. All the women were found because of tips to the police. All were in or near woods."

"The first one was found in a sewage drain."

"Yeah, but it was near some woods. The coroner said the first woman died approximately twenty-four hours before she was found, the second twelve hours, then...."

"What is it?"

"It's a Goddamn pattern. Twenty-four, then twelve, then six, then three—the last was just ninety minutes. We've got forty-five minutes this time. He's gonna inject Beth with the narcotic just forty-five minutes before he expects us to find her!"

"Hey. Carson."

Adam turned toward the door, his blood coursing with adrenaline. "Reggie boy said something interesting about his boy toy," Johnson told them. "Last time they talked, Pepper was bitching about his sugar momma making him jump through hoops to get his candy. He mentioned something to Reggie about having to get climbing gear."

"Climbing gear?" Adam began to see the orbits of clues rotate about a single possibility. "Hammer Rock! That's got to be it."

"Are you sure?" Red asked. "I mean the killer hasn't called yet to home us in on a location. This could be a wild goose chase."

"If we wait until he calls, it will be too late!" He snagged his coat off the chair and leapt for the door.

* * *

"Beth! Beth!" Adam screamed as he leaned over his unconscious wife. His finger quickly probed her throat for a carotid pulse. Her skin was white and cold, her breathing almost imperceptible. He had already given her two quick breaths. Please, Lord, please, he silently begged, please keep her alive. He forced himself to focus on finding a pulse.

Yes! A flicker of life still coursed through her veins.

He continued rescue breathing. A helicopter hovered overhead. Its spotlight suddenly illuminated them on the ledge.

"The chopper is going to send down a Medic." It was Red. She had scaled up the rock behind him. She knelt down beside the couple. "Is she alive?"

Resisting the urge to cradle Beth close, Adam nodded. He wasn't sure of her injuries. "I think she was drugged, liked the others."

Red pulled off her coat and laid it over Beth who was dressed in trousers and a sweater. She looked up as the chopper pilot called out over the PA. The Medic was lowered and Red helped her out of the harness. The woman quickly got to work. "I'm Lisa Cooper."

"Deputy Phillips and Detective Carson," said Red as Cooper began taking vitals. "The victim is Detective Carson's wife."

Cooper pulled out a vial and drew its contents into a syringe. "I'm going to give your wife two milligrams of Narcan." She addressed Adam but kept her eyes on what she was doing. Quickly and efficiently, she gave Beth the injection.

The litter was lowered and Red helped Cooper with the backboard and neck collar. They secured Beth into place and signaled the chopper to haul her up.

"We're taking her to the trauma center," Cooper said as she hooked herself back into the harness. She signaled the pilot and started up toward the chopper.

Still on his knees, Adam fought tears. "Did they get him?" he demanded.

Shivering now, Red shook her head. "Adam, you're hurt!" she cried out suddenly reaching for his ear.

"It's nothing," he told her but Red was already reaching into her jeans. She pulled out a tissue and gently dabbed at his ear, but the blood had already crusted over.

When she stopped, Adam put his face in his hands and sobbed silently. "She can't die. She can't die." He began to shake.

"It's okay, it's okay," Red soothed. She cradled his head against her shoulder as the helicopter soared off into the dark blue sky. "Shhh." Red rocked him, stroking his back as he sobbed. "I've got you. Shhh. She's going to be okay. The Narcan will counteract the Dilaudid. They'll take good care of her."

Adam let Red comfort him, but pulled away when a second helicopter arrived.

"Our ride," said Red.

*   *   *

Pepper did live in a dive. A visit to Big Ron's bar turned up a patron who knew where he crashed—a motel, the kind booking rooms by the hour. Adam insisted on leading the search after Bedard gave him the update. It had been a grueling night in the hospital, but the doctors said Beth was stable. The Narcan had worked. Now he was determined more than ever to find out who killed those women and who tried to kill his own wife.

The motel manager, a pear-shaped man in his sixties, puffed on a cigar as Adam questioned him. A heaping plate of pork fried rice sat steaming on the counter in front of him.

"Yup," he said in a frog-like voice. "I know him, but he don't call himself Pepper. Calls himself Potter, you know, like the sorcerer boy in the movies, but not Harry, Larry. He's been staying in Unit Thirteen for months."

"Is he here now?" Adam asked.

The manager shrugged. "Could be. I haven't seen him since yesterday morning, but that don't mean nothin'. He's gone for days at a time. Or he could be in there high as a kite."

"Let's take a look," said Johnson.

They walked around the backside of the motel. Adam pounded on the door. A greasy head popped out from the unit next door. "What in the hell is all the racket?" Bedard flashed him a badge. "Oh...sorry." He ducked his head back in and quickly shut the door.

"That a guy a regular?" Johnson asked the manager.

"Yup." He blew out a puff of smoke. "He drops in for some, ah...recreation now and again—different nights, different units."

Adams pounded again on Unit Thirteen's door. Johnson and Bedard pulled their weapons. "Open up! Police!"

"You got a key?" Johnson asked the manager. "I think I smell smoke."

"Yeah, yeah, yeah. You cops are always smelling smoke." He wobbled over to the door, put in a key, and turned the lock. "Help yourselves," he grumbled.

Adam pushed in the door and hit the light switch on the wall. Quickly, he scanned the room for signs of movement. The room was littered with dirty cups and the remnants of TV dinners. The bed was unmade, the dingy carpet stained and musty.

"Jesus Christ," Bedard gasped as he moved toward the bathroom. "Don't you have a friggin' maid?"

"Cleaning service for regulars is extra," the manager said from the doorway.

Adam moved toward the bathroom but gagged a few feet before the door.

"Holy shit!" said Bedard. He smelled it too. "Either there's something dead or something really rotten in there."

Adam pinched his nose momentarily before moving forward. He grabbed the door handle, but it was locked. Stepping back, he kicked in the door while Johnson and Bedard covered him.

Lying in the bathtub like a gutted fish in tomato soup was the body of Pepper, aka Larry Potter.

*   *   *

Adam knocked on the door. Red opened it without hesitation.

"Adam! Come in." Red smiled and took his hand. She led him into her tidy living room and gestured him to sit with her on her sleek leather couch. "How's Beth?"

"Good. She can come home in a few days."

"That's great." She leaned over and kissed his right cheek. "I'm so happy for you both. Anything more on Potter?"

Adam shook his head. "Nothing you don't know. We found fishing line, syringes, and the rifle he used to shoot at us." Adam absentmindedly reached for his ear. "Beth's ID confirmed him as her abductor, but we still got no motive."

"Does Beth remember anything else?"

"No. Potter rolled down the window of a black truck—he borrowed it from a motel neighbor, for consideration—and asked her if she was Beth Carson. Assuming he was Reggie Parks, she nodded and approached. Next thing she knew she was waking up in a hospital. We found a rag and ether in the motel room. He must have used it to knock her out at first. Funny thing, though."

"What's that?"

"Remember that Mustang that hit the old man's Impala by the grocery store?"

Red nodded. "We found one matching its description belonged to another acquaintance of Potter's."

Red shifted on the couch. "You still think Potter wasn't working alone?"

"Yeah. The Mustang owner has an airtight alibi and he says Potter borrowed his ride the night Grace Baughman was abducted. So if Potter was driving it to create a distraction, who grabbed Baughman? Or if Potter was the grabber, who was driving the Mustang?"

"Must have been somebody just paid for the job."

"Maybe." Adam shrugged. "We'll probably never know—just like the motive. Why did Potter kill those women and why did he slice up his wrists after he tired to kill Beth?"

"Maybe it was because he failed. We got there too fast this time. Who knows why these psychos do what they do? Besides, he deserved to die."

"You think so?"

"Why waste our tax dollars giving him a trial, lodging with three squares, and a free college education while he appeals the death penalty for fifteen years?" She suddenly drew in a breath. "The idiot almost killed you, Adam."

"Hey, Red, don't cry." Adam put an arm around her shoulders.

"I won't." She lifted a hand to wipe her eyes and then put her fingers into his hair. "I loved your dark curls from the moment I saw you."

Adam looked at her sheepishly. "When we were up on Hammer Rock and I fell apart, I…I…."

"Hey, I'm glad I was there for you." Her red brows rose. "What is it Adam?"

"I feel so guilty Red. I mean, my wife almost got killed and you were holding me and…well, for an instant I didn't want you to stop."

Her lips twitched as if she were holding back a smile. But she said somberly, "We're a great team Adam. You've been fighting you're feelings for me, because you're married…and I understand that." She took both of his hands and pressed them against her chest. "But isn't it worse to lie to yourself? Isn't it worse to deny your true feelings?"

Adam let her press his hands against her breasts. "I don't know."

"We can be discreet Adam…until Beth has recovered and you tell her about us."

Adam pulled back and stood. He walked over to her piano. He had forgotten she played. "There are too many obstacles, Red. It's better if we end this now."

"No." She moved up behind him and put her arms tightly around his waist, pressed her head into his back. "I won't let you go. I won't lose you!"

Adam ran his hands along the ivory keys. "Will you play for me?"

"I would do anything for you Adam." She released him and moved around him to sit on the bench.

Adam put his hands lightly on her shoulders as she smoothly tapped the keys. "Ode to Joy" filled the small apartment. Joy was far from what he was feeling, but he pushed on when she finished the song. "How do I know you'll stay with me if I leave Beth? How do I know I can trust you to never leave me, Red?"

Red stood and turned to look at him with wild eyes, her mask of normalcy slipping away. "Nothing will keep us apart; nothing <u>can</u> keep us apart."

"Tell me Red...Libby. Tell me how I can be sure." He put his palms on her cheeks. "I can't be with you, Libby, if I'm not sure."

Tears began streaming down her face. "I did it all for you Adam."

"What did you do for me?"

Red smiled through her tears. "I knew if we worked together, you'd notice me. You're so intense, Adam, when you're working—so focused. I wanted to be in that focus so badly—your focus. I arranged for an old acquaintance of mine to help me create a major case."

"Potter?"

"You're so smart Adam. Yes, Potter. I knew him from Chicago. He was multitalented—weightlifter, drug dealer, dominating sadist, on occasion. I just made use of his favorite hobbies. His sadism went too far and he killed the first victim. After that, more deaths didn't seem to matter. And, with each new case, you and I grew closer. In the end, his addiction made him unreliable and we don't need him anymore anyway."

"He killed those women. You <u>caused</u> him to kill those women."

"I did it for <u>you</u>, Adam." She threw her arms around him and clung. "I told you I'd do anything to be with you."

Adam held her, trying desperately to lock down on erupted emotions. "What about Beth?"

"Oh, Adam! Please understand," she pleaded.

"You knew Beth had been given Dilaudid. Some of the victims were dosed with Dilaudid, some with morphine. You knew which Beth had been given." He suddenly dropped his hands from her waist and grabbed her shoulders. He gave her a hard shake. "You knew because you instructed Potter to kidnap my wife and drug her! He dragged her up that rock on his back then left her there to die!"

"No! Larry wasn't supposed to give her so much—just enough to incapacitate her. Then I could take care of you and Hailey and show how good I am for you."

Unable to maintain the charade any longer, Adam's composure snapped. He slapped her so hard she tumbled to the ground, shocked and confused.

For an instant Adam stood over her and thought about wrapping his hands around her conniving, murderous throat. "Don't you dare say my daughter's name!" Adam shook his head in disgust just as two uniformed officers barged through the door.

"Read her her rights," he ordered.

"Adam!" Red shouted as he walked away. "Adam, don't leave me! DON'T LEAVE ME!" Adam stopped by the front door. He paused, knelt, and pulled the wire and transmitter from his ankle. Without looking back, he breathed deeply, tossed the bug on the sofa for the uniforms to retrieve, and strode into the sunlight.

*   *   *

"Adam, put me down. I can walk."

"Hush up. It makes me feel manly."

Beth giggled as Adam carried her through the front door and plopped her on the couch. "Does it make you feel manly to cook and clean for me too?"

"No." He kissed her on the forehead and turned as Hailey bounced through the door with his mother-in-law.

"Look, Mommy. We got more balloons!"

"They're beautiful! Thank you."

"Let's go put them up in your mommy's bedroom," said Joyce.

"Okay, Granny," Hailey said smiling and raced towards the steps.

Adam joined Beth on the couch and took her hand. It was so warm and alive. They sat quietly for a few minutes before Beth spoke. "Is Libby's lawyer going to use the insanity plea?"

Adam shrugged. "We can use the recording from when I was wired to claim premeditated murder. And it's only a matter of time before she cracks about Potter. The medical examiner is sure he didn't cut his own wrists."

"It's really sad. Hank told me how they found out she was abused and abandoned as a child. How terrible. Always needing love and willing to kill to get it."

"She needs to be locked up the rest of her life. I don't care if it's a cell or a mental institution."

"Adam."

Adam laughed. "You're amazing, you know that? Amazing and adorable."

His comment earned him a big kiss on the lips. He settled back onto the couch. "I've been thinking. It's a good time for me to go back to school."

Beth leaned forward, smiling. "Tell me more."

"I'm going to apply to law school. I just need a few more prerequisites, but I can take the classes in the evening. And if I get in, I can switch to nights."

"<u>When</u> you get in you mean. So instead of catching the bad guys—or girls—you're going to put them behind bars."

Adam nodded, gauging Beth's reaction.

"Sounds good to me," Beth said with a laugh. "Just don't ask me to do research for you. I get enough of that at work." She leaned over to kiss him as he laughed. "I've been thinking too."

"About what?"

"I've been thinking it's a good time to have another baby. Life is so precious Adam."

"God, I love you Beth." He pulled her into his arms and they clung to each other.

"Mommy! Daddy! Look!" Hailey was back downstairs jumping up and down by the bay window. "It's knowing!"

Adam and Beth turned on the couch to look out the window and smiled. The ground was already covered with a light dusting of snow.

Death can pay an unexpected call on anyone. The victims of the cold killers in "A Light Dusting of Snow" never doubted they'd grow old gracefully and comfortably until, perhaps, that last moment of helplessness and near-unconscious oblivion. To the young, ambitious, and busy, death seems a distant relative likely to visit only the infirm or old.

The frequently unexpected nature of death is a topic of this next tale as well. Harry and Goldie are friends despite their differences in age and philosophy. Fate brings a new character into their lives and disagreement into their relationship. Just when an agreeable resolution seems imminent, fate steps in again. This time, death is along for the ride.

Is life fair? "Harry and Goldie" will ask that question by its climax. We, naturally enough, ask it at the climax of our lives as well.

HARRY AND GOLDIE

by

Lucille Maurice Maistros

It was the usual Saturday night at the Cornerstone—*Fine Dining. Steaks, Chops, Seafood, Cocktails. Best Crab Cakes in Baltimore*—the night Goldie passed out.

The three-piece jazz combo in the corner of the lounge kept the volume notched down so as not to disturb the intimate conversations between the couples in the adjoining dining room. The aroma of grilled beef and fried shrimp drifted from the kitchen, blending with cigarette smoke from the bar where Harry leaned on his elbows, watching the crowd, silver hair shining in the neon glow, long legs stretched out behind him.

He liked tending bar. Now that he was alone, it filled the need to be around people, talk to them, get to know them. Much like his old job delivering mail. More interesting than assembling Big Macs at MacDonald's or greeting customers at Wal-Mart, as some of his fellow retirees were doing. *Of course, they didn't have to put up with cigarette smoke*, he thought, the SmokeEater humming overhead, *but there weren't as many smokers nowadays. A dying breed.*

"Hey, Mister, how about a drink?" she had asked, her short spiky hair a halo in the dim light of the Budweiser sign as she placed an empty tray on the service bar.

"Sure, what'll it be, kiddo!" he said, turning away from the line of half-filled liquor bottles shelved against the wall, his blue eyes framed by sun-creased skin wrinkled in smile lines suggesting he was about to tell you a joke.

"Two Merlots and two Chardonnays. It's going to be a wine night—might as well put the Jack Daniels away," she said.

"Fine by me," he said, reaching in one smooth motion for the bottles of Woodbridge and four wine goblets. "Makes it easy."

His practiced pouring filled the goblets exactly one inch from the top. He wiped the tray bottom quickly with the bar rag and placed the drinks on the tray.

"Thanks, Harry," she said as she turned toward the busy dining room. The sound of clinking water glasses and clacking cutlery grew suddenly louder as the jazz trio on the raised platform to his right took a break.

Harry reached below the bar and pulled out a food-warehouse-size plastic jar of pretzels and moved around the bar to refill the snack bowls. He emptied the only dirty ashtray. It sat in front of a well-dressed middle-aged couple that smiled guiltily at him, the stern warnings of the Surgeon General losing the battle with the need to feel young again, if only for an evening.

"How's that Chevy doing, Harry?" the man asked.

"Great!" How's that Mustang?" Harry asked as he replaced the ashtray.

"One hundred and sixty thousand miles and still running great," the man answered as his wife stubbed out her Marlboro. "We still take her out on weekends and drive her in some Fourth of July parades."

"She's a classic, alright, like us!" Harry agreed as he moved toward a man in a tweed blazer with elbow patches, an empty glass sitting on the green and white Heineken coaster in front of him.

"You ready to go home yet, Will?"

"No. I think I'll have another one. Please," he answered quietly, his red-rimmed eyes glancing up from their study of the bar-top.

"How long has it been for you?" Harry asked as the musky scotch swirled like an oil slick into the bottom of the glass. Harry added a little extra soda in what he knew was a futile effort to keep Will sober an extra minute or two. Looks like he'd be calling a cab for Will again tonight.

"Two years, last week. But you know," he added, lifting his eyes again, "it's like she just died yesterday."

"I know," said Harry. They were silent for a moment, each lost in his own memories.

"Well, then, how's the law treating you?" Harry asked, trying to change the subject.

"Oh, I'm sort of letting go of 'her majesty,' the law. My new partner's taking over a lot of the day-to-day. Just keeping busy with a few long-time clients who insist on 'the old man'."

"Just stay busy, Will, that's the secret—don't slow down or you'll rust out. You need to fill those empty corners."

"Yeah," he replied unconvincingly as he slid lower onto the back of the wooden stool and picked up the drink. Harry noticed the once-manicured nails now bitten to the quick.

Goldie was back, tray in one hand and order slip in the other.

"This four-top's a little more adventurous. They want two Bloody Marys, a Jack 'n ginger, and a rum and coke."

Was it the soft, white glow of the *Absolut* sign in front of her or something else that made her look so pale?

"You okay?" he asked.

"Just a little tired, that's all," she answered, her head resting on her slender hand. She watched him place a stalk of celery and a wedge of lime in each Bloody Mary.

"Maybe five nights is too much, with studying and classes," he said.

"Oh, I can handle it," she said. "Maybe I'm coming down with a cold or something." She lifted the tray from the bar and smiled at him as she turned toward the dining room.

"Poor kid," he thought as he watched her slender back retreating.

The only good thing about losing his Mary, if indeed, any good thing can come from losing your best friend of forty-two years, was that it had pushed him to get out and make new friends. Widows and widowers weren't too popular with their old, still-married friends, especially if the widower looked a little too much like an aging Paul Newman. He was friends with Vic, an ex-accountant, and Jim, a retired journalist, who sweated and grunted with him at the athletic club three times a week. Another friend, Barry, lived in the house next door when he wasn't living in a season-ticketed box seat at Camden Yards that he was more than happy to share with Harry.

And there were younger friends, like Goldie, who was kind to an "old guy" like him, having lost her own father when she was just on the threshold of puberty.

He turned to greet new customers as the band returned and the spiked tones of *Take Five* competed with the noise from the dining room.

Later, Goldie sat on a stool near the service bar, counting her tips and sipping a cup of coffee.

"How'd you make out tonight?" he asked, sliding crystal-clean wine goblets into the rack over his head.

"Oh, pretty good, actually," her long slender fingers sorting the bills by denomination. "Two hundred and forty smackaroos! Good thing 'cause the car payment's due next week." She put the folded bills carefully into an inside pocket of her worn leather shoulder bag.

"How about another cup of coffee?" he asked, leaning forward, elbows on the bar.

"Sure! Tomorrow's Sunday—I can sleep in."

"So, any new flames since Mike left?" he asked, pouring from the half-full carafe.

"No, I don't really have time, you know. Hey, how about you, mister? Are you busy tomorrow night?"

"Ask me again thirty years ago," he said, ruefully, both of them laughing at the familiar joke, although it didn't seem as funny now as it had a year ago, before they'd gotten to know each other.

Goldie looked away from those disturbing blue eyes. "Actually, with school and all, I don't have time. And it's better if there aren't any dates to cut into my tip time, you know?" her voice trailed off. *If you have more than one excuse*, he thought, *you don't have any.*

"So, have you decided what you're going to do when you graduate?"

"With the nursing shortage, I can pretty much write my own ticket. I'm thinking of applying to Hopkins. That would look pretty good on a resume, don't you think?"

"Absolutely," he answered, feeling a sudden stab of envy for her youth, her new career stretching away from her with endless possibilities.

"But what I'd really like to do, if it turns out that I like working in health care as much as I think I will, is to go back to school to become a nurse practitioner."

"Is that a new idea?"

"Not really. I've been reading up on it. Nurse practitioners have a lot of autonomy, almost as much as doctors. It's a definite trend in health care...I think I'd like it. Anyway, I'll see."

That's when she had looked up at him like a doe in a rifle's sight and slumped quietly to the bar, the high-backed stool keeping her from landing on the floor.

Harry quickly reached for her shoulders. Marty, the bass player, heading for the back exit, dropped his case and grabbed her arms from behind.

"Hey, wake up, little girl! What's the matter?" Marty cradled her carefully as Harry came around the bar and helped lower her to the floor. "Let's put her feet up," said Marty—bass player by night, EMT by day. Harry placed a clean dishtowel under her head. Nancy, the hostess, went for a glass of water as the two men crouched next to Goldie and tried to rouse her with their voices and gentle taps on the cheek. Harry dipped his handkerchief into the water and dabbed the back of her neck as Marty felt for a pulse.

"She's only fainted, thank goodness," Marty said.

"She doesn't do drugs, does she?" asked Nancy of no one in particular, her hands on her ample hips.

Finally, "What happened?" asked Goldie.

They helped her sit up. "Don't know. You passed out," said Harry. "How do you feel now?"

"Alright, I guess. Just a little woozy."

Nancy looked doubtful. "Well, now, don't try to stand up too quick, hon, it could happen again. We'd better get you to the ER. Better check you out. Maybe you're anemic."

"No, I don't think so. Anyway, I'll go to my own doctor as soon as I can. I promise."

Marty and Harry exchanged skeptical glances as they helped her to her feet. She still seemed weak.

"I'll be okay now. I'll just drink a little more water before I leave."

"Look, kid, you shouldn't drive," Harry said. "I can take you home. You don't have school tomorrow so you won't need your car too early. If one of your roommates can't bring you back here tomorrow to pick it up, give me a call. I'll be glad to do it whenever you're ready."

She started to argue but one look into his narrowed eyes and she knew she'd better say yes.

"That's right," agreed Marty, as he dusted off the knees of his otherwise impeccable slacks. "Better safe than sorry, babe."

Harry left the windows down in the '56 Chevy and Goldie leaned her head back onto the crackled vintage seat covers. The acrid odor of baked blacktop on the hot August street mingled with the wilted-salad aroma of overflowing trashcans as she watched white moths dance in the streetlights on Eastern Avenue.

"So, when's the baby due," Harry said quietly.

The back of her neck felt sticky as she turned it on the seatback and looked at him.

"I'm too tired to ask how you know," she answered. She could feel a thickening in her throat and tried to stop the tears.

"Is Mike the father?"

"Well, who else would it be?" she answered. With the mist in her eyes, the windshield suddenly blurred. "I'm sorry, I shouldn't take it out on you."

"Oh, that's alright. I guess you don't feel too hot right now. Or maybe, too hot is part of the problem. I have to get this air conditioner fixed. So what's Mike going to do about this?"

"He doesn't know. By the time we broke up in June, I knew I never wanted to marry him anyway. He has a new life in med school. And it's not as if I'm going to keep it. It's due in February but I'm not going to wait much longer. I'm just going to...you know...get rid of it. I hate to say it that way but, you know, it's not really a baby yet...."

"Now, Goldie, you know better than that. You're studying nursing, for Christ's sake!"

"Well, it's easy for you to feel that way! I mean, you're not the one that would have to take care of it. I want to finish school and, oh, this just spoils the hell out of everything!" She was sobbing pretty thoroughly now, hiccups and all.

He turned the blinker on and slowed for a right turn onto the street where she shared a brick row house with two other girls and a guy. Crickets chirped from a dozen tiny front lawns as he pulled up to the curb. He put the car in park and turned to her.

"Look, Goldie, I can't tell you what to do. But promise me you'll wait just a couple more days and think about it. Maybe there's another way out of this. I don't mean marrying Mike—you know, I didn't think he was good enough for you in the first place. But, you never know...maybe another answer will come along."

She put her shoulder against the door and leaned out into the night.

"I don't know. I just don't know. It would help if my folks were still around, but I probably wouldn't have told them anyway. I'll wait a couple days, like you said. I'm too tired right now to make plans. 'Night, Harry. Thanks for taking me home."

She smiled and turned toward the steps. He watched her until she went inside, turned on the front room light, and locked the aluminum screen door.

When the phone rang, she was sleeping so deeply she felt she had to climb out of a well to answer it.

"Hello."

"Goldie, it's Harry. Listen, I'm on my way over with breakfast."

"I'm not up yet. My roommates weren't here this morning to make any noise."

"Oh yes you are, I can tell. Besides, it's after twelve on a spectacular Sunday and you need to get some sunlight in those peepers of yours."

When his car pulled up, the inside door was open. He knocked on the aluminum screen door. "Come in!" she called from the kitchen. In cutoffs and a baggy Orioles t-shirt, she padded barefoot from the kitchen with two bright yellow mugs of coffee.

"You're really something, you know that?" she said.

"You sound like my Mary," he laughed.

They sat quietly together at the small dining room table, munching Egg McMuffins and sipping the coffee.

He cleared his throat.

"So, here's the deal," he began. "My whole life came this close," he pinched thumb and forefinger together, "to not happening. My mother didn't want me. She was an unwed mother. This was 1943. My father was her high school sweetheart until he graduated and then left for the Army Air Corps."

He pulled a handkerchief from his pocket, wiped his forehead, cleared his throat again and continued. "So, there she was. Didn't want to tell my grandparents. Didn't want to tell even her best friend or Father Vinci at St. Leo's. There were rumors about several girls in her neighborhood who had found themselves in a similar situation and who found a way to avoid having the baby. There was a midwife who lived upstairs over a pharmacy on Curley Street who would help girls with their 'problem.' But, obviously, she didn't do it. Instead, she told her parents. After they calmed down, they sent her to a Catholic girls' home where I was born. We lived with my grandparents until I was two. In 1945, she married the man I called Dad. My real father never expressed an interest in seeing me. He died piloting a B-29 in the Marianas in the South Pacific during World War II."

Harry paused for effect.

"And, so, here I am."

Goldie sat and traced the scratches on the tabletop with her index finger. She wouldn't meet his eyes.

"I want to help you out, kiddo, so you can have this baby and finish school. Mary had a good-size life insurance policy; the house is paid for and it's too big for me, by myself. It could use some young people to bring it back to life. You could move in for a while, have the baby. Then you can finish school and get yourself a decent job. You'll make it. You'll be okay. You just have to get through the next seven or eight months. And we can do it together."

She looked up. "I can't do that. I can't ask that of you. And, frankly, I'm scared. I've done my rotation in OB and let me tell you, having a baby does not look like a good time. So…thanks, but no thanks." She pushed herself from the scratched oak table and went back into the kitchen for the coffee carafe.

"No more coffee for me," Harry called after her. "I've got to go." He pushed himself from the table and stood up. Leaning against the kitchen doorframe, hands in the pockets of his jeans, he said, "I didn't mean any funny business you know. No strings attached."

Her eyes filled. "Of course I know that! I didn't mean to hurt your feelings. It's not about you, it's about me."

He left, closing the screen door softly behind him. She stood in the kitchen doorway, holding the coffee carafe, and looking at the empty spot at the table where he'd been sitting.

Monday came. She took her queasy stomach to class and it served as a reminder to ask one of the other students, Jen, who seemed to know everything about everything, to accompany her to the Family Planning Clinic. And she agreed. After class that afternoon they would go.

Another Saturday night but Goldie didn't show at the Cornerstone. With a sinking feeling, Harry heard that she had called in sick. *I'll bet she's sick,* he thought, sick himself at the thought. *Oh well, what're you going to do.* It wasn't 1943. Things were different today.

She showed up on Tuesday. Looking around, she asked, "Where's Harry?"

"In the hospital, hon. St. Joseph's," Nancy told her meeting her eyes over the stack of menus she carried in her arms. "They think he had a heart attack this morning."

He didn't look like himself, hooked up that way to so many wires, on Wednesday afternoon when Goldie walked into the ICU cubicle and moved slowly to his bedside. They would only allow her five minutes. His eyes opened.

"Well, you look like you've been to one heckuva party!" she said. He smiled. "Don't I wish!"

"What happened? I mean, you work out and all. You're in good shape for an 'old guy'! How could someone like you have a heart attack?"

"Well, just a bad gene I guess. And some clogged arteries. They're going to fix that tomorrow, though. Roto-Rooter those puppies." He coughed. "How're *you* feeling?" he asked, his tired eyes searching hers.

She reddened. "Not bad for a pregnant woman."

He closed his eyes and opened them again slowly. Everything felt like slow motion to him today. "Pregnant?"

"Yup. I kept thinking about what you said...and I...just couldn't go through with it."

"Well...first time a woman ever listened to me."

"Ha! I'll bet!" she laughed. Their eyes met and held for a moment.

"Well, they won't let me stay very long. Good luck tomorrow. I'll come back to see you after your surgery, Harry."

"Thanks. And thanks for the other thing, too. The offer still holds, you know."

"We'll talk about all that stuff after you feel better. I'd better go."

As she pulled aside the cubicle curtain and turned to look back at him, he was already asleep.

The phone was ringing as she unlocked the door after school on Thursday. It was Nancy. She was crying. "Harry's dead. He died. On the table," she sobbed. "He had an aneurysm...didn't make it through the surgery. I can't believe it." Goldie sank to the edge of her bed and felt the baby move for the first time.

When she arrived at St. Leo's on Saturday morning, her eyes scanned the large crowd for a familiar face. Nancy and Marty were there, sitting with Will and that older couple. Harry's friends Vic, Jim and Barry were in another pew. Goldie moved into the pew next to Nancy who was already clutching a damp handkerchief. "I can't believe he's really gone!" Nancy said. Goldie just stood and stared at the coffin in the front of the church.

Later, when it was all finally over and they were leaving the cemetery, she stood in the knot of strangers milling around their cars. Someone tapped her on the shoulder. Goldie turned to meet a pair of disturbingly blue eyes, crinkled at the corners. She felt a familiar warmth when he said, "You must be Goldie. Dad told me all about you." This young man, in his early thirties, smiled down at her. "I'm Dave. Your Harry was my Dad." Goldie burst into tears. They moved to a bench under a dogwood tree. "He was such a wonderful man!" she sobbed. "He'd do anything for anyone. Even me."

"I know, he told me. Told me about his plans. I feel like I already know you. Come on. Come on over to the house. We have a lot to talk about." He took her by the hand and they walked to a row of cars on the gravel path, his long legs taking shorter steps to match her pace.

"I'm going to name him Harry—if it's a boy," she said.

"He would have liked that," he agreed, placing her gently in the front seat of the funeral limo. "Dad would have liked that."

Authors and Artist:
Biographies and Backgrounds
(Listed Alphabetically)

Ann Cook

Ann Cook has lived in Harford County since 1942 and has only begun writing in her senior years. After a career in the computer field, she retired in 1990 and now spends her time writing fiction, traveling, and gardening.

She completed four semesters of Creative Writing at Harford Community College and has recently joined the Harford Writers Group. She enjoys the camaraderie of the entire group and the varied styles and experiences each member brings to his or her writing.

Her own writing is derived from her life experiences, dreams, and sheer and pleasant flights of imagination.

Mary Beth Creighton

Mary Beth Creighton is an aspiring novelist who has completed both a romance and a suspense manuscript. She is currently seeking publication of *Only a Matter of Time* and *The Elimination of Annie*. Mary Beth recently learned that *The Elimination of Annie* has won her second prize, suspense novel category, in the prestigious Maryland Writers Association writing competition.

Mary Beth is also the Director of Rehabilitative Services/Healing Arts Coordinator for Upper Chesapeake Health and has experience writing reports, proposals, and presentations. *Massage Magazine* just accepted one of her articles, a piece on hospital massage therapy, for future publication.

She recently has begun to enjoy writing short stories. The mother of three growing boys who inspire her daily, Mary Beth is married to her soul mate and best friend, Jerry. She enjoys spending time with her family, the outdoors, reading a variety of genres, and—of course—writing.

Lois W. Gilbert

Writers have always been encouraged to write about what they know. Lois W. Gilbert knows and loves her extended and diverse family and much of her work draws on the real events experienced by her many loved ones.

Lois grew up in Greenville, North Carolina and is a Southern woman at heart. In 1953 she moved to Maryland with her husband and raised five children here in the heart of the state. She is grandmother of fourteen and great grandmother of three.

Lois writes for the *Methodist Visitor*, a monthly publication of the Havre de Grace United Methodist Church. She has been published in the magazines *Plus* and *Mature Living*.

Karin Harrison

Karin Harrison was born in Germany. She came to the United States with a degree in business administration. While raising her three children, she worked for an optical company and attended college in the evening to become certified as an optician specializing in contact lens fitting. She wrote several technical articles subsequently published in trade journals in the United States and Canada. Karin has always been passionate about reading and continually nurtured a dream of writing.

Two years ago, she quit her job and enrolled at Harford Community College in Bel Air, Maryland where she completed Creative Writing.

Karin treasures the classics and derives much inspiration from the great authors. An ardent history buff, she particularly enjoys writing historical fiction. Currently, Karin enjoys two great avocations: fostering the growth of her writing talents and the growth of her two grandchildren. She and her husband live in Bel Air.

Danny L. Imwold

Danny L. Imwold teaches biology and marine biology in

Anne Arundel County, Maryland. A resident of Harford County for thirty years, he enjoys roller-blading, fishing, and writing. His first novel, the as-yet-unpublished *Sandsculptures*, is set on the Bimini Islands in the Caribbean. A science-based thriller, *Sandsculptures* places the reader on a beach that is both beautiful and menacing.

In addition to *Sandsculptures*, Mr. Imwold has been a featured contributor to *Canvasback* magazine and continues to write short stories in his free time. Despite his many interests and commitments, he is nearing completion of his second novel. Married with two children, Danny Imwold resides in Bel Air.

JoAnn M. Macdonald

Referring to herself as a "late bloomer," JoAnn Macdonald is a non-fiction writer and lives in Joppa, Maryland near the Chesapeake Bay. Her focus is on biographies of American women and on stories of public education.

Her inspiration to write began during her own high school years. Later, she began a teaching career at Joppatowne High School in 1973. However, the death of her young husband altered her life's plans for several years as she raised and supported her four young children.

Among her writing accomplishments is a biography of Antoinette Brown Blackwell, a section of which is anthologized here. The full biography was originally penned for the Unitarian Universalist Association.

Lucille Maurice Maistros

Lu was born and raised in St. Johnsbury in the scenic Northeast Kingdom of Vermont. The golden years of a carefree and happy childhood in that snowy but warm-hearted town are the memories she mines in her writing.

Her writing career began as editor of a local newspaper and shoppers' guide, the *Twin State Advertiser*, for which she also wrote a weekly column. She was the editor and writer of a monthly newsletter for the division of a multi-million dollar company, the J. M. Huber Corporation, headquartered in Edison,

New Jersey. She later served on the editorial staff of Huber's corporate newsletter and company magazine where she sharpened her interviewing, writing and editing skills.

Her summaries of technical papers have appeared in the *National Bureau of Economic Research Digest*. She prefers non-fiction and history, and her writing credits include healthcare topics for *Unique Opportunities*, as well as articles of historical interest for publications such as *Equilibrium*, the quarterly news magazine for the International Society of Antique Scale Collectors. She has received awards for her writing from *Writer's Digest* magazine.

Lu lives with her husband, Chris, in northeastern Maryland. Her first book, *Growing up Cold*, a humorous account of growing up in 1950's Vermont, was published in 2005.

K. Kellogg Smith

A lifelong aviation enthusiast and onetime private pilot, K. Kellogg Smith wrote "It's a Great Day for Flying" for a Harford Writers Group assignment to write a short story beginning with "*I knew I was in trouble when....*" The story came naturally to him. "Having trouble is something you know can happen when you're flying. It doesn't matter how, what, or when—you always prepare yourself to deal with trouble when it happens."

Smith's multifaceted background includes a tour in the Marine Corps and a career in communications electronics, programming, and technical writing and editing. His knowledge of radio communications sent him to sea for "fun and adventure" as a radio operator aboard cargo ships and oil tankers. Adventure he has had in plenty from being shipwrecked on a reef in the Philippine Sea to fighting pirates in South America.

Smith and his wife Doreen live in Abingdon, Maryland.

Frank Soul

Frank Soul was born in Harford County and raised in Carsin's Run, Maryland. Frank graduated from Bel Air High School in 1966 and has worked as a Maintenance Mechanic at CYTEC Engineering Materials (formerly American Cyanamid) for thirty-eight years. He hopes to retire after forty years of dedicated service and continuous hard work.

Frank also taught the Maryland Hunters Safety Program beginning in 1977 when it became mandatory to have the course to hunt in the state. Since that first class over twenty-eight years ago, he has taught over five thousand students the best practices for having fun, safe, and worthwhile experiences while stalking game.

His hunting experiences have spanned forty years in the wilds and woods of Western Maryland. He and his brother, Harry Gilbert (about whom many of the stories are told), have hunted Western Maryland since 1952. They have seen many changes, most made in the name of progress, but have also borne witness to an era of game and wilderness experience not likely to be seen in Maryland again.

James A. Vella

Jim Vella's passion for writing began in high school when Ms. London, his English teacher, read his paper to the class and then added, "I think this was copied from a book. Nevertheless, I gave it an A+ because young Mr. Vella at least <u>recognizes</u> a good descriptive essay when he sees one!"

Jim hadn't copied it at all. Although he should have been offended, perhaps, by the accusation, his reaction instead was quite positive. Jim recalls, "My chest inflated with pride...and I've been exhaling stories ever since!"

He's written a book of short stories and poems, six illustrated children's tales, and three novels (*Maybe Someday*, *Rachel and the Sylvan*, and *Roger: A Young Man's Odyssey to the Vietnam War)*. "Arcanum" is his first published short story.

Robin Wintz (our artist)

Robin Wintz, a banker by way of her aptitude for numbers and an artist through her creative talent, has loved drawing and painting since childhood. An avid boater, her paintings include many famous landmarks of the Chesapeake Bay including the Thomas Point lighthouse. She is also an active member of the National Society of Decorative Painters.

Although Robin uses the many beautiful landscapes across Maryland for much of her art, the characters of the stories dictated the illustrations in this anthology. She called upon her friends and family to model for these roles and to them, she dedicates the illustrations that grace these pages.

When Robin and her husband Tom are not at home in Fallston, they're at their second home, the navigable waters of the fair state of Maryland.

Charlotte R. Wrublewski

Charlotte Wrublewski considers herself a product of city and country—and not just one country. Although she grew up on the west side of Manhattan and attended New York City schools through adolescence, she moved years ago to what was then the small community of Abingdon, Maryland. She subsequently earned her bachelor's degree at Towson State University.

Her next life change was not city to town but country to country—specifically, she traveled to Poland to research her family and cultural heritage. While in Poland, she studied Polish language, literature, and history at the Jagiellonian University in Cracow. She has since made the history of Poland and its people a focus of her commitment to writing. Charlotte hopes to contribute to the preservation of the proud memories and traditions of her family and her ancestors.

Ted M. Zurinsky

After thirty-two years of teaching English, Ted looked for another use for his language skills and experience. Editing and writing have provided an interesting new challenge. Ted draws on his love of the mystery story, especially the police procedural, for many of his writing efforts. Many genres appeal to him, however, and this anthology offers a taste of nearly every one of them from autobiography to science fiction.

Ted has lived in the center of Harford County for nearly forty years and pursues interests in photography, golf, fishing, and travel—when he's not at the computer keyboard creating his own stories or helping others perfect theirs.

Printed in the United States
52645LVS00002B/145-426